Uncharted Territory

Ardent Redux Saga: Episode 3

Uncharted Territory

Ardent Redux Saga: Episode 3

By
J.L. Stowers

Editor: Keri Karandrakis
https://kerikarandrakis.com/

Cover Art: Tiffany at Dark Matter Book Covers
https://www.darkmatterbookcovers.com/

Visit the author's website at
www.jlstowers.com

DEDICATION

For my parents: Dennis and Beth.

Because raising me was a true journey into Uncharted Territory.

CHAPTER 1

Captain Dani Devereaux paced back and forth in front of the floor-to-ceiling display in *Osirion*'s bridge, stopping to examine the black, gelatinous mass slowly engulfing the *Raleigh*. "How about now?"

"Still nothing on the long-range scanners." Cassia Simpkins sighed, tossing herself back in her chair.

"Well, shit." Dani briskly made her way to Cassia's station, peering over her shoulder. "How long ago did you pick up the distress signal?"

"It started broadcasting about six hours ago, after we exited the wormhole. It's not the pre-recorded message we got earlier, just the standard distress signal any Galactic Conglomeratc ship can activate after systems failure when communication is not possible."

"That's activated manually. If someone's alive over there, shouldn't we do something?" Jag Reinhart was nose-to-nose with the image of the blob on the screen. "It looks like it's eating the ship."

Zadria Swift piped up from her corner, "That's not advisable. Protocol dictates we are to wait for our commanding ship to find us. Once *Houston* is here, I'm sure they'll know what to do."

"Except it might be too late by then," Dani mumbled as she rejoined Jag at the screen.

"There is a small airlock on the untouched side of the ship," Cassia said as she projected a detailed view through the holographic display.

Dani squinted at the docking bay. "It'd be tricky, even for the cruiser."

"I'm sure I could ease it in there. Zadria gave me a pretty good lesson," Jag said as he winked at her, which caused her to slouch down in her seat further.

Dani rolled her eyes and redirected her attention to Daemon Cruz. "Any idea what it is or where it came from?"

Uncharted Territory

"*No luck yet. Still researching,*" Cruz signed quickly before putting his head down and furiously typing away at his console.

Howard Glenn returned to the bridge with a tray of beverages and snacks. He carried a small bag of jerky over to Dani. "Here, eat this. You need to keep your energy up."

"Thanks, Howard." She accepted his offering and bit into the sweet, salty meat. "What do you make of this whole thing?"

"I don't want it on my ship, I can tell you that much." He nodded to the screen. "It's reaching to grab onto anything it can."

He was right. The black, churning blob was still pushing itself outward and away from the ship occasionally in an effort to reach Dani and her crew on the *Osirion*. She had purposefully kept them well out of range while maintaining control over the *Raleigh* by carefully alternating use of their gravitational beam and their thrusters.

Dani stared at the screen as she chewed. She wasn't sure what to do. On one hand, whoever sent the distress signal could still be alive. On the other hand, she couldn't risk contaminating her own ship or crew with whatever that thing was. Going for help was out of the question, too. *Osirion*'s gravity beam was the only thing keeping the *Raleigh* from drifting through space. If they tried to go anywhere, then who knew what would happen to the ship and its parasite? Besides, there was the fact that she was supposed to be dead and *Osirion* wasn't supposed to exist to complicate things. She sighed.

"You know what we need to do," Jag whispered at her side.

Dani nodded. She knew he was right. "You want to try your hand at flying *Osirion*?"

Jag shot her an angry look. "You know that's not what I meant. I'm not letting you go over there alone."

Dani stared into his eyes for a moment. His intense gaze let her know he wasn't kidding around. Jag was serious about protecting her after things went sideways with their first wormhole trip. "Zadria, Howard, are either of you capable of flying *Osirion*?"

"I spent some time on the simulator just in case a situation like this would arise. Patrick and I agreed it would be beneficial to have a backup." Howard placed his hand on her shoulder as he joined her to look out over the *Raleigh*.

"I've had far more hours in the simulator than Howard, but I'm not comfortable with this, at all." Zadria frowned.

Dani's eyes lingered on Zadria's face as she spoke before turning to Howard. "Thanks, Howard. You shouldn't need to do a whole lot, just keep the ship safe, don't get to close to that... whatever it is. We'll be back as soon as we can."

"*Good luck.*" Cruz gave an encouraging smile.

Cassia stepped over her therapy cat Carl, who was protesting as he looped around her legs. She hugged Dani and gave a reassuring smile. "Be safe and stay on the comms. Let us know what you need."

"Will do." Dani smiled as she looked around the bridge at her crew. She was lucky to have such an incredible team to work with. And, even though Zadria was reluctant, Dani was hopeful that she'd begin to mesh better as she learned more about how they operated.

"You ready?" Dani's eyes met Jag's once more. He seemed more at ease now that Dani had accepted his company, even though they had no idea what they were heading into.

"Absolutely," he replied without an ounce of fear.

They collected their comms and silently made their way down to the cruiser's docking hatch. Once inside, they helped each other suit up.

"Hey." Dani turned to Jag before he put his comm on. "Thanks."

Jag gave his familiar cheeky grin. "Oh come on, you knew this is how it was going to go. I'm surprised it took you so long."

Dani's smile faded and she bit the inside of her lip. When she worked for the Galactic Conglomerate, she was always the first one in on a rescue mission. In fact, she didn't usually even give it a second thought. But the destruction of her previous vessel, *Alaska's Vengeance,* her time in prison, and her 'execution' were taking their toll on her self-confidence. She wanted to make the right choices for everyone, but it was getting harder and harder to know what the right choices were.

Dani shook her head back and forth, trying to clear the self-doubt from her mind as they grabbed their helmets and slipped into the cruiser.

The cruiser itself wasn't very large. The exterior wasn't made of glowshard, like *Osirion*, but of standard issue Galactic Conglomerate materials. The theory was that building it out of standard materials would let them pass unnoticed among other similar ships should they need to dock or land anywhere. Inside there were six seats, two captain's chairs and two small benches along the side that could each hold two additional passengers. Between the benches was a small cargo hatch.

"I see why there wasn't room for more than two people when you went to pick up the trackers," Dani said as she slipped her comm device over her ear.

"Yeah, it's a bit cramped for sure." He turned on his comm and took his place at the controls.

Dani could have flown the cruiser herself; she quickly adapted to a variety of spacecraft. However, she hadn't done any test runs or simulation time for the craft, and their docking target was quite small. She was also thankful for the company, as she didn't know what was waiting for them on the other ship.

"Wait." Jag got up from his seat and climbed out of the cruiser, returning after a moment with two energy rifles and hand-held energy pistols.

"Just in case?" Dani asked.

"Just in case." Jag smiled and began the disengage protocol to loose them from *Osirion.* "*Osirion,* do you read?"

"Loud and clear," Howard's voice emitted from the speakers on the cruiser and in their comms.

"Disengaging now," Jag said as he lowered the ship away from *Osirion*'s belly.

As he slowly approached the *Raleigh* near the docking bay, Dani's eyes were locked on the organism that had now spread across three-quarters of the ship.

"I don't think we'll have much time in there," Dani said as it bubbled and stretched.

"We'll keep you updated on how it looks from the outside," Cassia reported over the comm.

Dani initiated a scan on the ship to try to get an idea for exactly which style of GC ship they were about to board. It was comparable in size to *Alaska's Vengeance*, but a sizable portion of the ship was missing while the rest was mostly obscured by the blob.

"No conclusive data and nothing on record about the interior design of the ship. I'm not getting any life signs under any of the exposed area, so if they're still alive I'm guessing they're under the obstructed part." Dani analyzed the situation. "Cassia, with the way this thing interferes with our scans, our comms may not work in there."

"Understood."

"Also," Dani continued, "If anything weird happens or if that thing comes after *Osirion*..."

"We know what to do," Cassia replied once more.

"Wait, what are we going to do?"

"Don't worry about it, Z." Dani smirked at the girl's innocence.

"Docking now," Jag announced as the nose of the cruiser started its way into *Raleigh*'s docking bay.

Dani sat quietly, not wanting to disturb Jag's concentration. There was little room for error at the small airlock. She cringed as the cruiser jolted, then exhaled a sigh of relief as it shifted, locking into place. "Okay, we're docked. Heading in."

The pair stood and armed themselves. They each holstered a handgun before picking up a rifle.

"You ready to do this?" Jag asked, clicking off the safety on his weapon.

"I'll take point," she said, slipping her helmet on. "Looks like oxygen levels are minimal in there."

Jag popped his helmet on as well, nodding to her.

Dani opened the cruiser's hatch, then climbed through into the small airlock. Once inside, she opened the door to the rest of the ship. A portable console on her wrist showed her that oxygen levels on this side of the airlock door were higher, but not ideal. She signaled for Jag to follow her.

It didn't take long for Dani to get a feel for the ship's layout. She had been on this model before. They quietly trudged down the hall, looking in each room along the way.

"Seems odd that all the doors are open. They must have been locked that way," Jag's voice came through the communications device in the helmet.

"Cassia, can you still read us?"

"There's some feedback, but yes, for the most part. It looks quiet from out here."

"Okay, let's try to pick up the pace. I'm getting a bad feeling." Dani's instincts were screaming for them to get back to the cruiser, but she couldn't leave anyone on this ship to die. Not after what happened in PS683.

"We've got a body in here," Jag said, stepping into one of the private quarters on the ship. "Or what's left of one anyway. It looks kind of... deflated."

Dani watched from the doorway as he crouched down to the figure, which looked more like a discarded glove than a human, and scanned it with the port-con. "How long?"

"Not long. Maybe a few days." Jag grabbed the arm and tried to roll the body over, but he quickly withdrew his hands as the body rippled and fell back down face first with a splat. A light green fluid started oozing from the mouth, nose, eyes, and ears. He stood and walked back toward the door, gagging in his helmet. "Okay, I'm not looking for identification. That is disgusting."

"I'm sure it smells lovely, too." Dani stared in horror as the body's contents continued to spill out onto the floor. "Let's move on."

The light from Dani's rifle swept into the next doorway, the kitchen. It looked much like the one on *Alaska's Vengeance* had after passing through the wormhole, except two crumpled bodies lay on the floor. She again guarded the door, watching the hall as Jag entered and scanned the bodies.

"Same on these," he said, shaking his head. "Not long at all."

"Shit," Dani mumbled to herself. Ships of this size didn't usually have more than eight people on board, and they'd already found nearly half the crew dead.

Dani continued down the hall to the next room. Her senses were magnified in the dark silence. The only sounds she heard were Jag's breathing and her own breath and pulse. She found herself stepping with each heartbeat, slow, steady. Her eyes were quick to take in every object her light cruised over.

Uncharted Territory

The bridge should be up ahead, she thought, and from what she could remember of the exterior, it would be directly underneath the black blobby thing. "Cassia, do you read?"

No response.

"I think we're on our own, boss," Jag's soft voice wafted through her helmet.

Dani proceeded toward the bridge, directing her light across the ceiling, floors, and walls before her. Finally, it landed on the door to the bridge. She entered the standard GC override code onto the control panel, but it didn't move.

"The door to the bridge is sealed," she observed out loud, finding it a bit peculiar when all others were open.

"You better see if anyone's home, because I don't think we should hang out much longer."

"Creeping you out, is it?" She chuckled softly, trying to cover up her own discomfort about their situation.

"Well, that, and that black crap is inside the ship."

Dani spun to face Jag, whose light shone down the intersecting hall. Along the floors, wall, and ceiling, the ooze rolled toward them, glacier-like. It bubbled up and extended where the light hit its jelly-like surface.

"Get the light off of it!" she barked under her breath before sprinting to the bridge door.

She banged on the door with the bottom of her fist, hoping that someone was still in there and she wasn't risking their lives for nothing.

"It's getting faster." Jag's voice quivered ever so slightly.

Dani glanced over her shoulder as she continued to bang on the door. He was keeping his light ahead of the blob, but just barely. She was tempted to tell him to turn it off, but figured it'd be better to see it than to not see it at all. *Come on*, she thought as she kicked the door repeatedly.

Finally, the door shuddered and slid open. A man in a space suit stood before her, two more behind him. They looked utterly bewildered to see her. Dani beckoned them to follow her, but they didn't move. She rolled her eyes and grabbed the closest man by the wrist, yanking him out of the bridge.

"Jag, these guys are in shock or something. Help me get them to the cruiser."

Jag backed toward them, still keeping his light trained on the hall as the ooze neared the intersection. He gave the man a shove and pointed down the hall they entered the ship from. That seemed to be enough to get him going.

Dani swung her rifle over her shoulder, grabbing the other two and hauling them out of the bridge. *"Is this it? Are there more of you?"* she signed.

She sighed and shook her head at the lack of response. All GC crewmembers were taught sign language to help in situations where verbal communication wasn't possible. However, the crew of the *Raleigh* wasn't even responding to that. Dani grabbed each of them and towed them down the hall after her. They passed through the intersection as the ooze started to pool out of the hall behind them. It was still picking up speed.

"Cassia, can you read?" Dani said, urgently. "This crap is crazy. Can you see it moving on your scanners? Is the cruiser still clear?"

"Oh thank goodness, I was afraid we lost you. Cruiser's good, and yeah, that ooze has a unique signature. I can see your and Jag's life signatures coming down the hall—is it chasing you?"

"Yeah, it is. It's not fast, but it's creepy as hell." Jag laughed as he shined his light back toward the ooze behind Dani.

"Wait." Dani stopped in her tracks, letting go of the men and swinging the rifle off her back and into her hands. "Just me and Jag?"

"Yeah, the two of you. Why?" Cassia started to sound a little worried through the comm.

Dani's heart jumped into her throat as her eyes met Jag's in the illuminated helmet display.

"Because we're not alone." Jag's voice was as cold as the blood pumping through her veins.

Dani's attention turned to the two men beside her. She took another look at their dopey expressions. They were pale—too pale. She lifted the light from her rifle up to the face of the man closest to her, the skin rippling as the light hit it. Green liquid started dripping from the gaped mouth.

Uncharted Territory

"Oh, that's sick." Jag's retch came through the comm, making Dani's stomach do a turn.

A few quick jabs at her port-con confirmed it. They were dead, too. She started backing away from the men, keeping her rifle trained on them. "Get back to the cruiser."

Jag shoved the man next to him toward the other two. He collided into the others, causing the three of them to fall to the floor.

Dani and Jag took the opportunity to make a run for it, bolting back down the hall toward the hatch while the mess of limbs and suits tried to get back to its feet.

She glanced over her shoulder, then turned, continuing down the hall backward, rifle trained on the men who were now pursuing them. Their movements were awkward and slow, but steady. A noise from the room beside her startled her. A quick flash of her light showed the two crewmembers in the kitchen were clamoring to their feet.

Dani turned to sprint toward the hatch, swinging it open and diving inside, Jag right

17

behind her. As soon as he was clear, she swung it shut and sealed it. "Go, go, go!"

Jag jumped into the pilot's seat and quickly disengaged from the airlock, the cruiser parting from the *Raleigh*.

Dani watched in horror from the small viewing window as the men didn't stop their pursuit at the airlock. They pushed themselves out into open space, flailing their arms and legs as they floated toward the cruiser. "Jag! Get us out of here!"

The cruiser shot forward as he engaged the thrusters, causing Dani to topple and roll across the floor. She made it to her feet and got to her seat, collapsing into it, taking off her helmet and shaking her hair loose.

Clear from the *Raleigh*, Jag took his helmet off too and stared at her. "What in hell was that?"

Dani shook her head, and opened her mouth to speak, but no words came out.

"Are you guys okay?" Cassia's voice shouted through their comms, causing them both to flinch. She had been asking about their status since they realized they weren't in good company, but they had ignored her.

"Yeah, yeah. I think so. That was... something else." Dani sighed and closed her eyes as Jag steered them back toward *Osirion*.

"Halt your approach," Zadria ordered.

"What? No." Jag shook his head and rolled his eyes.

"Given what we just heard, I can't let you board. I can't even let you near *Osirion*."

"She's kidding, right?" Jag turned to Dani.

Dani hesitated a moment. They did come in contact with the organism, maybe not directly, but it was all around them and in the *Raleigh*'s crew. Dani shuddered as she visualized oozing green bodily fluids. "No, she's right."

Jag slowed the cruiser to a drift. "Care to share?"

"We don't know what that stuff was or what it's capable of. I mean, there were dead people walking around on that ship."

"Right, I was there."

"We've been exposed. We can't risk infecting the crew, or the ship for that matter. Glowshard, remember? It's alive."

Jag groaned and slumped back in his seat.

"Understood, *Osirion*. We'll sit tight," Dani reported back. "Any word from the *Houston*?"

"Not yet," Cassia mumbled. "You can't just stay out there. You don't have any rations."

"Hey." Dani smiled at Jag as she replied to Cassia, "We'll be fine."

Dani muted her comm and then the cruiser dash comm so *Osirion* wouldn't be able to hear their conversation, then Jag did the same with his.

"Hey, looks like we might be out here a while," she started. "Thanks for coming with me on this totally horrifying waste of time."

Jag laughed. "Anytime. Though maybe we leave the black oozy stuff alone from here on out?"

"Agreed."

"You know, there's one thing I don't understand." Jag turned toward her, scratching his head.

Dani raised her eyebrows. "Just *one* thing?"

"Heh, right?" He flashed his charming smile. "But if they're all dead, who sent the distress signal?"

Dani sat upright, a moment of panic running through her body. "Do you think we missed someone?"

"Well, I'm just saying, if a black space ooze creature was walking around in people suits, maybe I'd stay hidden." Jag shrugged. "I dunno, maybe I'm overthinking it."

"Yeah, maybe." Dani stared out the window at the *Raleigh* and the zombie-like humans floating near the airlock. She wondered if she had been too careless. What if someone was alive on that ship and she missed it? They hadn't looked everywhere. It was completely possible that someone triggered the distress signal and hid in the ducts or a cupboard somewhere. Still, she couldn't risk Jag's life on a 'maybe.'

"I see those wheels turning, missy. You better knock that off. I didn't mean to send you into a spiral."

Dani attempted a half-hearted smile.

"Look, Dani, I've been meaning to talk to you about something..." Jag trailed off, looking down at his hands.

"Guys, we just picked up the *Houston* on the long-range scanners. They're out of our ICC zone, but I sent them our location." Cassia's cheeriness was a relief.

"Oh, sweet." Jag grinned.

"Wait, what were you wanting to tell me?" Dani furrowed her brow.

"Oh, don't worry about it. It can wait." He winked and sat up straight, peering out the windshield.

They spent the next few minutes in silence until a brilliant flash appeared near *Osirion.* As soon as their eyes recovered from the bright light, they could see the *Houston* and all its glory, instantly making *Osirion* seem like a toy.

"You think Patrick will be mad?" Jag turned to her.

"Probably," Dani answered.

Jag laughed. "Excellent."

Dani couldn't help but smile and shake her head.

"What have you done?" Patrick's voice projected anger even through the comm.

"Here we go." Dani sighed and reached over to unmute them.

"It took you long enough." Dani smirked.

Patrick laughed. "Alright, now that we got that out of the way... well done."

Jag and Dani exchanged a confused glance.

"We're downloading the data report right now. I have analysts standing by to review it. I hear you encountered an alien organism?"

"That's right," Dani said. "And, if you direct your attention to that ship over there and the crewmen flapping around it, you'll see it firsthand."

"I'll have our team analyze the organism as soon as we get you and your crew taken care of."

"Also, I have a few questions. First of all, why was there another GC shi—"

"There will be plenty of time for questions after we analyze the data."

Dani shook her fist at the speaker when Patrick interrupted her, causing Jag to laugh.

"Jag, you sound like you made it through okay. Greeeaaaaat." The sarcasm spilled from the speakers.

"Sorry to disappoint, boss man. Can't get rid of me that easy, you know."

Patrick sighed audibly through the speaker. "Okay, Jag, please bring the cruiser around to Dock 4. We'll have a decontamination crew waiting for you there. *Osirion* will fall into orbit around *Houston* until the two of you are able to return."

"Copy." Dani wrinkled her nose at the thought of having to spend more time on the *Houston.*

"Oh, and congratulations. Out."

"What a tool," Jag said as he grabbed the controls once more.

"I heard that." Patrick sounded less than enthused.

Dani reached over and slapped the mute button on the microphone just as they laughed up a storm.

As Jag neared Dock 4, another ship departed. Through the windshield they could see four fully suited crewmembers. Dani and Jag shared another concerned look before he eased the ship into the dock.

As promised, a full decontamination crew was standing by. Their blocky-looking decontamination suits made their movements awkward.

Uncharted Territory

"Now the real fun begins," Jag said as he shut down the engines and took his hands off the controls.

The decontamination crew misted the outside of the cruiser with a pink-tinged fog. As the fog settled, there was a bang on the cruiser's hatch. Dani opened the door and the man offered her his gloved hand. She accepted and climbed out of the ship.

Once Jag was out, a few members of the decontamination crew climbed inside the ship while Dani and Jag were escorted through a ribbed, plastic tunnel and into a sterilized room. Inside were two twin-sized beds, a private bathroom, and a kitchenette.

"Wait." Dani turned back to look through the glass wall. "How long are we going to be in here?"

Patrick stood on the opposite side of the glass, outside of the tunnel they'd just used. "We aren't sure yet. Once we have a better analysis we'll let you know."

Dani pursed her lips and nodded reluctantly. "Fine."

"Dibs!" Jag shouted as he quickly removed his space suit and jumped onto one of the beds.

Dani stared at the crumpled suit lying on the ground and shook her head, trying to rid her mind of the bodies on *Raleigh*. Instead, she tried to picture them alive, which only made her more curious about them.

"So, Patrick, tell me about the *Raleigh*," Dani said as she slipped out of her space suit and placed it in a bin.

Patrick sighed and began pacing back and forth in front of the glass. "The *Raleigh* was the first ship to attempt wormhole travel after your happy accident."

Dani frowned. "I don't know that I'd call the hell I went through a happy accident."

Patrick held up his hand and continued pacing. "Irrelevant. They actually entered from this side, here in PS505. We didn't realize the wormhole we sent you into was the other end of this one."

Jag joined them at the window after scooping up his suit and tossing it in the bin on top of Dani's.

Patrick sighed. "When we failed to find them, we feared the worst. It appears as though the organism attacked their ship mere days after it entered the wormhole."

"Wait." Dani stepped closer to the glass. "What are you basing that assumption on?"

Patrick stopped pacing and looked at her, perplexed. "Why, the data we downloaded from *Raleigh* of course. Systems show there was a significant impact causing extensive damage to the ship shortly after they entered the wormhole. The alien organism then began to eat away at the ship after four days."

Dani and Jag shared a lingering look of confusion.

"What now?" Patrick folded his arms over his chest.

"When we came through the wormhole, the organism hadn't reached the *Raleigh*," Dani said slowly, still working through the statement in her head. "The ship was trapped alongside a massive asteroid."

"Which I blew up," Jag interrupted.

"Right," Dani continued. "It was only after we freed it that it encountered the organism."

Patrick looked from Dani down to his port-con, punching in the information. "That doesn't make sense. It must have had an encounter before you arrived."

"How long has the *Raleigh* been missing?" Jag asked.

"Nearly six full GC months."

"When do *Raleigh's* logs show they entered the wormhole?" Dani craned her neck in an attempt to see the data he was looking at.

Patrick sighed and tapped the port-con a few more times, then he froze. His finger poised above the screen, he slowly raised his eyes to Dani's face. "Four days ago."

The three stared at each other momentarily before Patrick turned and walked away, leaving Jag and Dani alone.

"Weird." Jag scrunched up his face.

Dani folded her arms over her chest, watching the door Patrick exited through, hopeful he'd come back soon with an explanation. "I don't like this, one bit."

CHAPTER 2

"You're making my neck tired." Jag sighed from where he sat on his bed, arms folded across his chest.

Dani stopped and glanced down at the floor. There was a considerable difference in the amount of shine along the path she had been pacing. "Oh..."

"Right. Oh." Jag stood and walked over to Dani, grabbing her firmly by the shoulders. "You need to relax."

"But—"

"No buts. Now, I'm sure there's something more entertaining to do in here than watching you wear a groove in the floor." Jag started digging through the cabinets.

Dani huffed and looked around the quarantine cell. She was starting to feel as though she were a prisoner constantly getting transferred from one cell to another.

She longed for the hint of freedom she was afforded on her ship and loathed the bland white interior of the *Houston* more than ever.

"Here we go, chess." Jag smiled as he withdrew the game from the cupboard and carried it toward Dani. "Oh now what is it?"

"I just hate not knowing things. Patrick hasn't given us an update in several hours and I need to know what's going on."

Jag set up the board and pieces. "Well, maybe a friendly game will help get your mind off of things."

She watched as he placed the pawns and power pieces in their designated places. This wasn't the first time they had played, but it had been quite some time since their last match. Jag almost always beat her, often boasting about how easy chess is to win if the player fully understands the value each piece brings to the board and doesn't mind the occasional sacrifice.

A few moves into their game and Dani's mind began to wander again. She wondered how the rest of the crew was holding up on *Osirion* and if the orbit around the *Houston* was as dull as it was inside.

"It's your move."

Uncharted Territory

Dani blinked rapidly, bringing the board back into focus. "I'm sorry, I just can't concentrate."

"That's what you say every time it looks like I'm going to win." He winked.

Dani managed a smile and got up from the table, stretching. "I wish they'd let us out of here. I hate not being able to see the stars."

Jag nodded. "I hear you there. Why don't you try to get some rest? I'll wake you if anyone comes by."

Dani yawned; it wasn't a bad idea. She had barely slept since the quarantine began. The bed felt like a lumpy pile of month-old rations and smelled about the same. But it was softer than the floor, and that was her only other option. Dani crawled into bed and stared up at the overhead light. "Is there any way to turn that thing off?"

Jag looked around the room. "Afraid not. I don't see any switches. But... hang on."

Dani watched curiously as Jag rifled through the cabinets and drawers before coming up with some tape. He slipped the dark blue pillowcase off of his pillow and used a pen to puncture holes in the thin fabric. After removing the chessboard, he climbed onto the table and taped the pillowcase over the light.

"Your stars, m'lady," he said with a deep bow, nearly toppling off of the table.

Dani laughed. The pillowcase didn't block all of the light, but it did a fantastic job at dimming the room. The holes in the fabric resembled distant stars and brought a smile to her face. "Clever. Thank you."

Jag smiled, pleased with himself, and fell onto his own bed, folding his hands behind his head, staring up at his creation.

Dani closed her eyes and slowed her breathing, attempting to will her body to sleep. She had gotten pretty good at a type of self-hypnosis to fall asleep quickly, an important skill when her insomnia grew bothersome. Starting with her feet, she began to relax, slipping into unconsciousness before she even reached her knees.

Her eyes got heavy and she started to feel as though she was drifting weightlessly through space. It took her a moment to get her bearings, but there she was, floating among the space dust at S802-P825-C1106-66d.

Uncharted Territory

Dani swam through the waterless sea of dark silence. Then, something caught her eye. A glinting metal object drifted toward her, spinning in slow motion as it neared. A signet ring. *Could it be?* As the ring completed its rotation, a boldly carved 'D' circled around to face Dani. Her thoughts echoed in the void around her as though they, too, were part of space. She reached for her father's ring, stretching her fingers out as far as she could reach, but not far enough.

She did everything she could to accelerate toward the ring as it passed by her, just out of reach, and continued on its orbit. Dani kicked, thrashing her legs and arms in an effort to get purchase on something, anything. But the blackness closed in on her, holding her, pulling her back into suffocating darkness.

"Dani." Jag clawed at the blankets that Dani had managed to tightly wrap herself in during her dream. "Calm down or I can't get you out."

She managed to tear the fabric away from her face, her hair clinging to her jawline from the static electricity. Gasping for air, she stared at Jag, bewildered, forgetting for a moment where she was.

"Must have been some dream," Jag said, helping her into a seated position as he knelt next to her bed. "You alright?"

"Uh, yeah. I think so." Dani smoothed her hair back down before rubbing her hands over her face, starting at the bridge of her nose and working in an outward circle until they stopped over her mouth. She exhaled deeply, the warmth of her breath pushing out between her fingers. Before she could fully gather her thoughts, a tapping came from the glass.

Patrick stood on the opposite side of the glass with two doctors, drumming on the pane with his knuckle. "Wrap it up, lovebirds. Let's get you out of here."

"We're clear?" Jag said as he stood and approached the glass.

Dani pushed herself to her feet, hesitating a moment to make sure her wobbly legs were going to do their job, and joined them.

"Yes. Our research indicates that the organism is only interested in necrotic tissue and is generally inert to all else."

"So, dead stuff," Jag clarified.

Patrick sighed and rolled his eyes. "Yes, 'dead stuff,' which means the crew must have expired on impact after their entry into the wormhole, before the organism latched on to the craft."

"Expired? They're people, not yogurt." Jag glared at Patrick through the glass.

"Look, I think we all understand what everyone means. We're not dead, so we're not at risk." Dani took a step closer to the glass. "But explain how it reanimated their bodies and sent the distress signal."

"As far as we can tell"—Patrick shrugged,—"it produces an electrical charge as a byproduct. The charge is enough to temporarily resume motor functions in a deceased lifeform, and possibly enough to activate the distress signal, but not enough to send an actual message."

"Okay, what about the difference in time?" she asked.

"We'll have to look into it. We still don't have a whole lot of data to go off of right now. We're comparing the data from the *Raleigh* with *Osirion*'s recordings. What we've seen so far indicates that travel from one end of the wormhole to the other was instantaneous for *Osirion*; however, that was clearly not the case. Nor was *Raleigh* only in there for four days."

"That brings us to the most important question of all." Jag's eyes widened.

Patrick looked at Jag curiously. "What's that?"

"Why are we still in here?"

Dani couldn't help but laugh as Patrick's face fell in disappointment. She had caught the familiar glimmer in Jag's eye and chose not to speak up, instead letting Patrick take the setup.

Jag maintained his charming grin as Patrick called for a guard to unlock the containment unit.

"The cruiser has been cleared and resupplied. You're free to join the others on *Osirion*," Patrick rattled off the statement before briskly walking from the room.

Dani turned and raised her eyebrows at Jag.

"What?" He shrugged.

"Nothing, let's get out of here."

Patrick wasn't joking about the supplies. Dani and Jag had to squeeze through the boxes to get to their seats on the cruiser. The cargo hatch was full, as was the rest of the small craft. Jag expertly maneuvered the ship toward *Osirion* as Dani read over the supply list.

"Anything good?" Jag asked out of the corner of his mouth.

"Nothing that stands out. Basic supplies, food, the usual." She was slightly disappointed that no other luxury dinners would be happening in the future, but she was also happy about the resupply because it meant they wouldn't be reboarding *Houston* for a while.

Dani sighed and tucked the list back into one of the boxes while Jag docked the cruiser on *Osirion*'s underbelly. "Excited to be back?"

"Oh, sure, but it wasn't so bad."

Dani arched an eyebrow at him.

"I mean, sure, the goo and dead people weren't ideal. But other than that, I was in good company."

"So, you're building a bond with Patrick then?" Dani winked and joked.

"Oh, sure, you know, always a people pleaser."

Dani was amused and curious about the red hue that settled on Jag's cheeks but didn't have time to joke about it as a banging on the hatch interrupted her thoughts. Dani hopped up and opened the hatch to see a beaming Cruz.

Cruz motioned for Dani to hand him a box and she complied. He then passed it off to Zadria, who passed it to either Cassia or Howard depending on the contents. It only took a few minutes to empty the contents of the cruiser.

When Dani finally climbed out, everything was neatly sorted and stacked. "Nice work, team. Do you mind storing all of this while I hit the showers? It's for everyone's benefit... trust me."

"I better go, too," Jag said, following Dani before stopping and turning to Zadria. "I mean, to shower, alone, by myself, in a different stall of course."

Dani rolled her eyes and shook her head, proceeding up to the main deck.

Once they reached the bathroom, Dani stepped into a private stall and turned on the water. The facilities in their cell on the *Houston* had provided the ability for them to clean themselves up a bit, but they hadn't had access to the bathing facilities.

Advances in technology offered a variety of shower options on *Osirion*, but Dani still preferred a good old-fashioned water shower. There was something so soothing about the steady stream of warm water that helped her relax. She often did a lot of thinking in the shower and enjoyed the alone time.

As Jag started belting out a song in his own separate stall, Dani's mind snaked back around to her strange dream. Not only did a complete stranger and a mysterious crewmember want her to visit that specific area of space, but now her own subconscious did as well. Dani stepped further into the water, letting it run down her face as she thought.

Dani had been to S802-P825-C1106-66d once, not long after the incident. Seeing the wreckage was enough to ensure she'd never return. As a result, she had spent the better part of her life avoiding that location, but now her curiosity was piqued once more. Since the scans hadn't been updated, the only way to know for sure what was out there was to visit the area itself. However, it was so remote that any venture that direction would surely raise red flags.

Dani quickly washed, rinsing the conditioner from her hair just as the water clicked off. She dried her face and shook her head, trying to rid her mind of the coordinates. For all she knew, it could be a trap anyway.

Moments later, she was dried, dressed, and entering the bridge.

"Captain on the bridge," Zadria announced, standing.

"Please," Dani said, raising a hand. "That's not necessary."

She was thankful that she had broken the rest of the crew of their traditional GC formality training early on and hoped Zadria would soon follow suit. Dani always viewed her crew as her equals more than her subordinates, despite warnings that they would walk all over her. They never disobeyed a direct order without good reason, and Dani believed that was due to a mutual respect among them. When they had hesitated in the past, they'd typically had sound reasoning against her decision;

however, they also trusted her to do what she believed was right.

Jag had already beaten her to the bridge and was fiddling with the controls on the holographic display, randomly shrinking and expanding the *Houston* as though it were a holographic yo-yo. Dani's cocked eyebrow eventually caught his attention, and his hands slinked back from the controls.

"What's next on the agenda?" Dani asked as she and Jag took their seats, her eyes glancing around the bridge.

"While you were in quarantine, they made a few improvements to the trackers," Howard began. "They've adjusted the launch settings so the trackers will stay closer to *Osirion*, within the shields. They also amplified their signal considerably."

Dani nodded. "Seems like good news."

"The amplified signals now have the potential to get picked up by other ships, however."

"I see." Dani pursed her lips. "Well, if that's a problem, we'll handle it then. What else?"

Howard grinned. "They also gave us a drone to—"

"A drone, you say?" Jag perked up.

Howard glared at him for interrupting, then continued, "The drone will help us place the stabilization units. The idea is that together they'll stabilize the entrance or exit of the wormhole, while acting as a door."

"A door?" Dani wrinkled her brow in an attempt to wrap her mind around the science behind their function.

"If I may?" Howard had approached the display podium.

Dani nodded and leaned forward.

Howard brought up a holographic image of the wormhole they'd emerged from the previous day. "We'll fly the drone around the perimeter of the wormhole's entrance to place the SUs."

"Wait." Jag held his hands up and grinned. "Who will fly the drone?"

Howard sighed. "Me. I'll fly the drone."

"Oh." Jag sunk back down in his chair, clearly unpleased with the answer.

"Go on." Dani nodded back to the display.

"Anyway..." Howard hesitated, eyeing Jag momentarily before turning back to the display. "I'll place the SUs around the mouth of the wormhole. The energy field they create will prevent the wormhole from collapsing in on itself while generating a conic shield. Only ships with the standard GC shielding frequency will be able to pass through. All others will simply be deflected around the entrance, hence the outward cone shape. Don't want anyone slamming into it."

"But, the GC shielding frequency changes often." Cassia had her stylus and tablet out, jotting down notes.

"Yes, these will update the same way GC ships do."

Cassia nodded, doodling wildly with one hand and absentmindedly scratching Carl between the ears with the other.

"They want us to place these on each end of the wormhole." Howard blipped off the display as he finished.

"So, if I'm understanding this correctly..." Dani folded her arms over her chest, watching Howard return to his seat. "They're wanting us to limit access to the wormholes for others?"

"Yes," Zadria chimed in. "Wormholes are notoriously unstable, and we don't know how long the SUs will be able to counteract that. We wouldn't want a civilian ship to travel into a wormhole and get stuck... or worse. They also allow us to monitor which ships are using which wormholes, which is important on many levels."

Dani's eyes shot around to her, Cassia, then Jag, and finally landing on Cruz's worried face. Her eyes lingered on his a moment and he quickly signed, "*Later.*"

Dani nodded and looked back toward Zadria. "When do we start the new protocol?"

Zadria smiled. "Now, actually. They want us to stabilize this end of the wormhole, then fly back through and do the other end with the improved trackers. *Houston* will be leaving as soon as I give them the green light. They're going to use their FTL drive to try to meet or beat us to the other end."

Dani smiled. "Sounds like a challenge. Wormhole versus a GC faster-than-light drive. I can see why they want us to succeed. Stable wormhole travel will be extremely beneficial to the GC, saving time and money spent on fuel as well as engine wear and tear."

"Alright!" Jag hollered from his seat. "The race is on!"

Regret and worry spread across Zadria's face at Jag's enthusiasm before she nodded and wordlessly lowered herself into her chair.

Dani navigated *Osirion* closer to the wormhole as the bright flash of *Houston*'s departure filled the aft cam. "Alright, Howard, you're up."

Howard rose from his seat, retrieving the drone's control interface from a cupboard.

Jag craned in his chair, attempting to get a better look at the device as Howard sat once more, locking the interface onto his console.

Once Howard was locked in, Dani focused her attention on the wormhole ahead. She absentmindedly watched the drone approach the mouth as she ran through the obstacles she remembered from her first pass. With the asteroid and the *Raleigh* out of the picture, she was confident that their journey would run smoothly.

As Howard carefully placed the SUs around the mouth of the wormhole, a red laser ran from device to device. Once they were all in place, they emitted a second red beam out toward *Osirion*, casting a red, glowing cone. Dani was impressed with the technology and turned to Jag to find him still pouting. She shook her head with a smirk before looking back toward the red, web-like structure of lasers.

"So, what's to keep someone from just taking one of those out and disrupting the whole system?" She flopped her wrist backward, finger extended toward the screen.

"The net can function with as few as three SUs. If someone were to take one or more of them out, the wormhole would become significantly less stable. If a ship were to attempt to enter the wormhole after disabling the net, then there's a ninety-eight percent chance that it will collapse immediately."

Dani nodded, trying to hide her concern with the system. It seemed like there were too many things that could go wrong. Hopefully, since *Alaska's Vengeance* was still the only known spacecraft to survive a wormhole, attempts for wormhole travel would be minimal.

"SUs in place and the net is activated," Howard stated with pride.

Uncharted Territory

"Alright team." Dani took one more look around the bridge. "Who's ready to head back in?"

CHAPTER 3

"Jag, get those new trackers out there," Dani ordered as she eyed the net of lasers wearily.

He grinned and took aim with his controls. However, rather than a burst and the deployment of a high-speed tracker orb, the ball merely exited and floated slightly away from *Osirion*. "Wait, that's it?"

Howard snickered at his disappointment.

"Don't forget the one in the back," Zadria added.

"Already done." Jag sighed and slumped into his chair.

"What?" Zadria looked at her console. "Oh, I didn't notice."

A deep chuckle rolled out of Howard, and Jag looked even more hurt.

Dani shook her head, trying to rid the smirk from her face. "I'm heading in."

She slowly guided *Osirion* into the net of lasers and held her breath. Thankfully, the ship passed through them easily, the lasers acting as a mere lightshow on *Osirion*'s shields. Once the better part of the ship was inside the wormhole, the current took hold.

The second time through was much less challenging. Dani had a keen memory for where the obstacles lay. There was no blob, no *Raleigh*, and no difficulties on their journey back through. In fact, the crew seemed bored with the journey. Dani focused on the course ahead, but could see Jag spinning in his chair out of the corner of her eye. Cruz and Cassia seemed to be signing back and forth, but Dani didn't want to eavesdrop and kept her eyes on the road.

They emerged from the other side with both tracking orbs intact.

"Looks like the adjustments to the trackers worked like a charm," Zadria beamed.

Dani nodded. "Well done, but I don't see the *Houston*."

"Guess that means we won," Jag said.

Uncharted Territory

"By my calculations, it will arrive shortly," Cruz signed.

"Alright, well, in the meantime, Howard... do your thing."

Dani set the thrusters to hold them in place at the mouth of the wormhole so Howard could install the SUs on this end. "Zadria, keep an eye on things. Notify me immediately if anything changes. I'm running to the galley."

"Yes, Captain," Zadria said, standing and taking the captain's chair.

Dani caught Jag's puzzled eye and nodded for him to join her.

"Trying to keep me away from the helm?" Jag sounded annoyed as soon as the door to the bridge slid shut behind them.

"Of course not. I just want to hear your opinion on all of this." Dani gestured over her shoulder to the bridge as they walked toward the kitchen.

"Well, I mean, the trackers aren't as exciting now," he complained as he poured himself a cup of coffee.

"What about the nets?"

Jag shrugged and poured a second cup, passing it to Dani. "Makes sense that they wouldn't want anyone getting in there and getting hurt."

"Maybe." Dani nodded a quick thanks. "I just don't know about this. The GC already controls so much. It just seems like another way to hold power over the people."

"Don't forget that we're in the middle of a war. A quickly shifting war at that. They wouldn't want civilians flying into the middle of a battle. You know how quickly the Vaerians moved into PS683."

Dani cringed at the mention of PS683.

"Can't say that I blame you, honestly. The GC ran you through the ringer," he continued as he put his arm around her shoulders, giving a reassuring squeeze. "You're bound to be a little paranoid, right?"

Dani sighed. "I guess."

Jag immediately dropped his arm from around her as they heard footsteps approaching.

Dani rolled her eyes and grabbed a third cup, filling it as Cruz walked into the room.

"*We have to talk,*" he signed after taking a swig of coffee and setting the mug on the table. "*I patched into the GC news transmissions while you were in quarantine. There have been some developments."*

"Go on," Dani said, sliding into a seat at the table.

"The ship responsible for the destruction of PS683 was traced back to the rebel sector."

Dani stared at him a moment, allowing the words to sink in.

"Wait," Jag interrupted with a hushed voice. "So, it wasn't Vaerian forces then?"

"No, it was a Vaerian ship, but it turns out it was stolen by the GC rebels."

"How'd they piece that together?" Dani whispered.

"They caught a rebel spy who confessed."

"How... convenient." Jag's eyes met Dani's.

"So, let me get this straight," Dani started. "The rebel sector has existed as long as I remember. They've never done anything like this before. Usually they're just sabotaging ships and space stations, mildly annoying stuff. So how do they go from being a nuisance to destroying an entire planetary system and millions of innocents, not to mention a rebel refugee planet? That's quite a leap."

"Wait, there was a rebel planet in PS683? Why do you know this and I don't?" Jag furrowed his brow.

"You learn things in prison." Dani shrugged. "I don't think the rebels would do this."

Cruz shrugged. *"I only know what was being reported. But, there's more. They said Dani had joined the rebel sector and was working with them for the destruction of PS683."*

"Well, as far as they know, we're all dead now. So, no harm done, right?" Jag grinned.

"Not exactly. As far as they knew, Cassia and I were still around, and Howard is off being 'officially' retired."

"I can already see where this is going." Dani rubbed her temples.

"Reports say we're being brought in for questioning."

"I guess we better have a chat with Patrick when he shows up then."

Zadria's voice rang out on the comm system, "The *Houston* has arrived."

"Talk about timing," Dani said as the three of them stood.

54

Uncharted Territory

She briskly made her way back to the bridge after finishing her coffee, Jag and Cruz trailing behind.

"Net looks good, Howard," Dani praised him as she took the captain's seat once more. Zadria scuttled back to her station.

"Incoming transmission," Cassia announced.

"Alright, half-screen please." Dani sat up straight in her chair, waiting.

Patrick's face filled the screen. "We need you to dock for immediate transport to the next mission location." His face blipped away just as quickly as it had appeared.

Confused glances bounced from crewmember to crewmember as they all strapped in.

Dani maneuvered *Osirion* to effortlessly glide into its original docking bay. The launch propulsion system caught the ship as it gently slid in and lowered to the floor just before Dani engaged the localized gravity. As soon as *Osirion* was parked, *Houston* crewmembers flooded the hangar. Storage doors were opened, consoles rolled out, and lifts extracted crates and approached *Osirion*.

Dani raised her eyebrows, visibly impressed with the pit crew–like choreography.

"Alright, crew, let's go stretch our legs." Dani stood and led the way off the ship through the loading ramp. As soon as she did, workers filled the ship and began checking their inventory with tablets in hand.

"Kind of nice that we don't have to restock ourselves, but didn't we just do this? Do we really need more stuff already?" Jag folded his arms over his chest and surveyed the activity.

Dani caught sight of the stars outside of the bay's hatch as they streaked and blurred. The *Houston* was making a jump.

"Well done on securing your first target." Patrick approached the group, arms out as a welcome.

"In a bit of a hurry, are we?" Dani nodded toward her ship.

"The next distance to the next wormhole exceeds *Osirion*'s jump capabilities. It's more efficient for us to take you there, while we restock your ship."

"We're pretty well stocked already," Jag mentioned as he watched another crate roll by.

"Yes, well, we want to make sure you have plenty of supplies in case you aren't able to get back to us in a timely manner."

Jag hesitated and studied Patrick's face. "Planning for the worst, are we?"

"You know, you could just throw a better jump drive in there." Dani folded her arms over her chest. "It'd solve the problem of us waiting around for you to find us."

Patrick just stared at her in response before turning on his heel and walking away.

"So, do you suppose that's a 'yes'?" Jag asked from behind her.

"Highly unlikely," Howard countered.

"I still don't trust that guy," Jag announced with a sigh.

Dani expected to have her idea shot down, especially with the recent developments of the alleged rebel ties; still, she had to ask. She also shared Jag's sentiments about the suspicious overloading of supplies. She reached out and snatched a tablet out of the hands of a worker as he walked by.

J. L. Stowers

"I need to make a few adjustments to the supply list," she said as she glanced over the items.

The worker pointed her in the direction of his supervisor before going about his tasks.

"I have some things to take care of." Dani waved back at her crew as she started making her way toward the supervisor.

The supply list was rather well done, but she needed an excuse to break off on her own a bit and gather her thoughts. She also wanted to track down Patrick and find out how he planned to handle the whole rebel fugitive angle that the news was blasting across the galaxy.

Dani stopped at the supervisor and mentioned a few more things for the supply list, including some high quality food and a few games for entertainment. If they were going to be gone a longer time, then she wanted to make sure they'd have more than prepared meals and boredom to keep them going. The supervisor jerked the tablet out of Dani's hands and rolled his eyes at the additions before waving over another worker and pulling him aside.

Uncharted Territory

Dani glanced across the hangar at her crew. Cassia and Cruz were deep in conversation again. They seemed to have a lot to talk about these days. Meanwhile, Zadria seemed unimpressed about whatever tale Jag was telling that required him to gesture wildly. Howard watched the pair, his belly bouncing up and down as he chuckled.

"Okay, well, we can get most of this, but we don't have any hupnal steaks to spare." The supervisor seemed annoyed.

Dani cocked an eyebrow at the man, unsure if there was a distinct shortage of hupnal steak aboard or if he just didn't think they deserved any more of the delicacy. A quick glance around the hangar indicated there was little else for Dani to do after speaking with the supervisor, so she took the opportunity to step out of the hangar and into the boring white halls of the *Houston* in search of Patrick.

Dani made her way briskly through the halls in search of Patrick but was disappointed that she couldn't find him in any of his typical locations. In fact, the rest of the *Houston* seemed unusually quiet outside of *Osirion*'s hangar.

"You there," Dani hollered after a guard walking down an intersecting hallway. "Do you know where Patrick is?"

The guard's eyes shifted quickly in the direction in which he was going. "He should be in Conference Room D."

Dani thanked the guard and wound back to the conference rooms, wondering what could possibly make the GC guard so uneasy. The door was closed when she got there, and Patrick's strong, commanding voice spoke out behind it. Dani couldn't quite hear what he was saying and leaned in close, but the speech stopped just as she did. The door suddenly slid open, and Dani was face to face with one of the ship's scientists, who startled and jumped back, nearly causing an avalanche of lab coats.

"Sorry," she mumbled as she stepped aside to let them exit.

After the last scientist stepped out of the conference room, Patrick greeted her in the doorway, looking perturbed. "Yes?"

"Can we talk?"

"I suppose so." Patrick stepped aside and swept his arm toward the table.

Uncharted Territory

Dani quickly took a seat and racked her brain for a starting point.

Patrick sighed, checking the clock on the tabletop display.

"So, rumor has it that the rebel sector was responsible for PS683?"

"Mmhmm." Patrick leaned back in his chair, pressing his fingertips together as he narrowed his eyes at her.

"First they say one thing, now they say the rebels. Seems like they're grasping at straws anymore."

Patrick continued to squint at her silently.

Dani wrinkled her brow at his response. "What should we do?"

"There's nothing to be done," Patrick spat out the words like they left a bad taste in his mouth.

Dani pursed her lips and glanced across the tabletop display. "You don't think they'll come after Cruz, Cassia, or Howard?"

Patrick shook his head with a slight smirk. "They probably will, but, naturally, they won't find them."

"You aren't worried about anyone on this ship saying anything? I mean, some of the staff isn't exactly friendly."

"You and your crew don't have anything to worry about here. *Houston*'s entire crew is invested in this project, besides..." Patrick leaned forward in his chair, lowering his voice. "I know *everything* that happens on this ship. Plus, everyone here has something to lose."

Dani nodded slowly. "Okay. And I'm guessing you're hauling us halfway across the galaxy to get us out of the way, just in case?"

Patrick smiled. "You can never be too careful. The *Houston* has a massive ICC field. This particular wormhole places some distance between us and the closest police outpost. We'd have plenty of time to react if someone were foolish enough to attempt to go over my head."

"I'm counting on you to keep us all safe." Dani hated to admit it, but it was true.

Patrick stood and placed a fatherly hand on Dani's shoulder. "You worry about keeping your crew in line and getting those missions done. Let me worry about everything else."

For a moment, Dani felt as though Patrick were channeling her own father. His sturdy hand, his way of making her feel safe.

Her expression gave away her doubt. "I'm serious," Patrick said once more. "I know you feel as though you were wronged for what happened before, but I'm not going to let anything like that happen to you."

Dani opened her mouth to talk, but Patrick turned her and guided her into the hall.

"Please, get back to the hangar and prep your crew. We're nearly there." Patrick took a step back, the door to the conference room closing between them.

Dani remained there in the hall, staring at the door for a moment. This wasn't the first door closed in her face, but that didn't reduce her worry. More times than not when this sort of thing happened, it was because someone was hiding something. Regardless, there was nothing she could do about it right now. Her cheeks billowed out in a long exhale before she turned and headed back to the hangar.

When she arrived, the others had regrouped and were waiting for her. Stars still blurred past the window, but the new supplies had been loaded, the empty crates removed from *Osirion*'s hull, and the hangar was cleared.

"Howard," Dani said as she approached the group, "did you check everything over yourself, too?"

Howard nodded. "Everything looked great. Nothing out of the ordinary."

"Good." Dani breathed a sigh of relief. "Patrick tells me we're almost there. Let's board and get ready."
Dani led the crew up Osirion's ramp once more, thankful for the retreat into her ship.

CHAPTER 4

Dani drummed her fingertips on the arm of her captain's chair as she waited for everyone to get settled in. Carl, attracted by the noise, jumped up into her lap, curled up in a ball, and started purring.

"You're quite the little anxiety detector, aren't you, Carl?" Dani whispered to the feline as she rubbed his cheek with her finger.

Carl rolled onto his back and pawed at the comm hanging from Dani's ear.

"What's our next mission, Z?" she asked as she placed the comm back in her ear to protect it from Carl's claws.

"They want us to set up the net then head in and see wherc it goes," Zadria answered, swiping across the tablet that held her notes.

Carl, displeased that Dani removed his toy, hopped down and made his way to Cassia's side. She quickly scooped him up, and he curled up in her lap.

"Any surprises in this one?" Jag asked as he flipped between status screens on his console.

"I hope not." Zadria sighed as she wrinkled her forehead.

"I'm actually kind of liking not knowing where we're going to end up. Keeps things interesting," Cruz signed with a smile.

"I'm not so worried about where we're going to end up as what's going to happen on the way there." Zadria's voice cracked, and Carl perked up his ears.

Dani saw the stars outside *Houston* come to a halt through *Osirion*'s windshield and perked up. "Looks like we're here."

"Alright, the hangar's clear. Go ahead and head out when you're ready. Good luck," Patrick said to the crew through the comm.

Dani grabbed the controls and proceeded to launch *Osirion* out into the open space around the *Houston*. The wormhole, suspended in space, was immediately visible after *Osirion* left the safety of *Houston*'s belly.

Dani began a scan of the wormhole and accessed the holographic display. Only, instead of the wormhole, the display zoomed in on the coordinates of S802-P825-C1106-66d.

A gasp escaped Dani's lips as the familiar scene unfolded on the holographic podium before her. Immediately her eyes darted to Cruz, who held up his hands defensively. Her hands were frozen above the controls, but the scene still managed to shift to that of the wormhole before them.

"Wait, what was that?" Zadria asked, standing.

"Malfunction," Jag quickly retorted, giving Dani a tight-lipped nod while Zadria examined the podium.

The rest of the crew seemed to be sharing concerned glances, but Dani did her best to avoid any further eye contact and she instead focused on the wormhole projected on the holographic display.

The outer edge of this one was far more flattened than the previous two. In fact, the beauty of it helped bring Dani back to the present. It looked like a blossoming clematis, her mother's favorite flower.

"It's so pretty," Cassia cooed as Dani brought *Osirion* around to face the funnel head on.

Petals of pink and silver bloomed open from the center of the funnel and reached into the darkness of space around it. The hollow of the tunnel lacked the glowing white light they'd experienced before, but the pink and silver continued down the throat, illuminating the first bend.

"Howard?" Dani cued without taking her eyes off the beauty before her.

The bridge was silent.

Dani blinked rapidly and pulled her eyes from the wormhole. "Howard?" she asked again, turning to look back at the gawking man.

"Oh," Howard mumbled as he shook his head back and forth. "Right, sorry."

"What are we going to name this one, Jag?" Dani turned to him and nodded toward the wormhole.

"Oh, I don't know, maybe Claudia."

"What? Not impressed?" Cassia asked.

"I've seen prettier things." He shrugged.

Dani almost swore she could see a red tinge creep across Jag's face as he angled his neck to stare down at his console controls. She turned and raised an eyebrow to Cassia, who shrugged in return. She then looked to Cruz, who she noticed was glancing at Cassia out of the corner of his eye. *What is going on with my crew?* she wondered.

The drone launched, and Howard expertly guided it around the petals, placing each SU carefully around the rim. "If the other end is as large as this one, we'll need to restock on SUs before the next mission."

"I'll make a note," Zadria commented as she tapped on the screen of her tablet.

Dani still wasn't sure about Zadria, but it was nice to have another person around to take care of things. Standard GC crews ran with four individuals, the captain, first officer, communications officer, and navigation specialist. Warships like *Alaska's Vengeance* also carried a doctor, mechanic, a weapons specialist, and a crew of fighter pilots and alternates. However, with the pressing war drawing out resources, Dani's previous crew lacked a weapons specialist and alternate pilots. Still, they'd managed to make a decent dent in Vaerian forces.

Now, her crew looked somewhat different. Jag doubled as first officer and weapons specialist as he did before. Cruz now carried the additional title of medic, as did Zadria and Cassia to a certain extent. Howard's duties had now stretched beyond those of a mechanic. It seemed that they were all working multiple jobs at this point.

"All set," Howard announced as the net linked and came online. The cone of this wormhole was much flatter due to the outer shape of the funnel, but it still looked like it was functioning properly.

"Alright, everyone ready?" Dani asked as she ran her regular systems checks, ensuring everything was ready to go.

Nods around the bridge satisfied her question, and she slowly maneuvered *Osirion* into the net. "Don't forget our tracker orbs," Dani reminded Jag.

"Launching now," he replied.

Dani verified the tracker orbs on her monitors before proceeding forward. "*Houston*, we're proceeding into the wormhole now."

Uncharted Territory

"You've got a go from us. All systems are up and tracking. Take care," Patrick's voice confirmed.

The moment before the wormhole took hold of them with its own gravitational pull was exciting. It reminded Dani of the time her father had taken her off-world to a planet boasting a large amusement park. She remembered anxiously looking at her father as they sat in the front car of an old-fashioned roller coaster. The climb to the apex of the track was filled with anticipation of the ride ahead.

As *Osirion* continued to creep forward, Dani felt the current-like gravity catch. "Here we go!"

She eased up on the thrusters, letting the wormhole do the work to conserve fuel. The tunnel ahead looked clear of debris up to the first bend. As soon as *Osirion* was past the point of no return, the gravitational force took hold, lurching the ship forward and into the tunnel.

The brilliant pinks and silvers continued as they sped through the wide space. This one was much roomier than the wormholes they had traveled before. It was almost an enjoyable experience. The beauty combined with the ease of the flight made it seem like they were out for a leisurely drive.

"Well, this one doesn't seem bad at all," Zadria said, sitting up a little taller in her seat.

"No." Jag pointed across the bridge at her. "Never, ever say that."

"What? There isn't anything in here that poses a threat," she replied, gesturing to the windshield ahead of them.

"Radiation levels are spiking," Cassia announced.

"Close the solar shades," Dani ordered.

"*That's* why." Jag quickly pressed the switch to close the solar shades and activate the display screen before sitting back in his seat, crossing his arms across his chest with a smug grin.

Zadria shrugged. "So? Radiation is to be expected in wormholes. In all honesty, the solar shades should have already been closed prior to entering."

Dani sighed. "Enough bickering, you two. It's done now. How are we looking, Cassia?"

"Good. The solar shades effectively stopped the radiation."

Uncharted Territory

Dani relaxed her shoulders and continued to guide *Osirion* through the bends of the wormhole. It did feel almost too easy, but she didn't dare say anything, as the universe loved to prove her wrong.

"Detecting massive lifeform readings ahead," Cassia said as she squinted at her monitor.

"Weird," Zadria mumbled as she stared down the straightaway projected onto the large screen. "I don't see anything but the end of the tunnel."

The long, straight section of the wormhole ended with a small, black circle in the distance, much like the exits of previous wormholes. Dani peered ahead. "You sure, Cassia?"

"Uh..." Cassia pecked at her console rapidly. "I don't think that's the end, Dani."

As the wormhole continued to pull them through the tunnel, Dani couldn't help but notice that she couldn't see anything defining in the darkness ahead. In the other wormhole, there had been a glimpse of stars and whatever else lay on the other side. Not this time. Just pure blackness.

"Shit," Dani muttered as she realized what lay before them. "Jag, weapons, now."

Jag offered a puzzled look but complied with the order, lowering the weapons relay to his console. The relay controlled four sets of primary weapons located around the ship, as well as eight additional minor weapons. "What am I aiming at?"

"The ooze ahead that's completely blocking the tunnel." Dani's blood chilled as she gave the instructions. She hoped that the weapons would have an effect on the roadblock ahead, because she knew the shields wouldn't protect them. The shields were only designed to protect against energy blasts and projectiles. They weren't capable of offering a bubble of protection through however much of the black, oozing organism lay in wait ahead of them.

Jag fired into the dark that spanned the width and height of the tunnel. The energy blasts poked holes through the organism, but they quickly filled again with more of the churning ooze. "This isn't working. It's like shooting mud."

"Keep firing!" Dani ordered, racking her brain for an alternative.

Uncharted Territory

As they drew closer, they could see that the ooze had coated the inside of the wormhole, not only blocking their path but also spreading like roots down all sides toward them. "How thick, Cassia?"

"It's thick, more than four times the length of our ship," she replied as she projected the results of the scan on the holographic display.

Dani knew they couldn't fly through the mass. The density would likely result in an unsurvivable collision, and even if that didn't kill them, the organism would lock onto their ship and they'd have no way to rid themselves of it. With as much as they measured, they'd likely remain stuck in the middle of it with no way to seek help. "Prepare to hop," Dani ordered.

"Wait, you're going to hop while *inside* a wormhole?" Zadria's vitals immediately elevated. "You realize that we have *no idea* what will happen, right?"

Dani ignored her, knowing it was their only chance. "Jag, reroute weapons power to the jump drive."

"Yes, *Captain*." He enunciated the last word and shot Zadria a dirty look.

Dani couldn't help but smirk slightly as she started up the jump drive, the hum of it vibrating throughout *Osirion*. She'd never let them know, but she preferred the bickering over the flirting any day. The organism ahead seemed to be pulling itself through the tunnel toward them, the roots getting thicker as it drew closer before thinning out further down the tunnel.

"Here we go!" Dani activated the jump drive, causing the wormhole around them to jolt. A tendril of black reached toward them from the middle of the tunnel just as the walls of the wormhole fell away into a blur of pink, silver, and then black.

Osirion rattled and shook violently, alarms sounding throughout the bridge.

"Shields are dropping rapidly," Jag announced, his words thick with worry. "Seventy-five, sixty, forty-five, twenty percent."

The light radiating around them from the main screen changed from blackness to blinding yellow light, prompting Dani to drop out of the hop.

"Shit!" Dani yelled as space slowed around them and they found themselves heading into a massive yellow star. She banked *Osirion* away from the gigantic celestial body, firing the main engines and the secondary thrusters to full power in an effort to break out of the star's gravitational pull.

"Shields are at twelve percent," Jag advised.

"Hull temperature rising to dangerous levels," Cassia echoed the temperature alarm sounding and flashing through the bridge.

Dani couldn't respond, as all her strength and attention was focused on not flying into the star. Unable to directly break the gravitational pull, she instead decided to slingshot around the star. She only hoped that she could do it before the ship was entirely compromised.

Using the star's own gravity, Dani shot around the equator with incredible speed. In fact, readings indicated that they were traveling much faster than the engines were equipped to handle due to the momentum from the wormhole, the jump, and the star's gravity.

A large solar flare erupted before them, reaching out into space and nearly into their path. The heat could be felt throughout the bridge as sweat streamed down from Dani's forehead.

"Shields at four percent," Jag announced.

Almost there. Dani stared ahead as they completed the slingshot and escaped the star's orbit, flying away from it into a planetary system thick with a significant number of worlds. A sigh escaped Dani's lips as they sped past the molten planets closely orbiting the star. There were upwards of two dozen planets locked in orbit around the star at varying distances and orbits.

"Temperature dropping," Cassia announced with a sigh of relief.

Dani quickly glanced at the vitals display, levels for all crewmembers dropping to normal ranges. "How did we come out on shields, Jag?"

"Two percent. That was close. The damn star just about burned away everything we had."

Two percent was still better than zero, Dani rationalized with herself. "Cruz, see if you can pinpoint our location. I'm going to slow us down and fall into orbit around that larger planet at one o'clock."

Uncharted Territory

The bell dinged and Dani guided *Osirion* to the deep blue and purple planet ahead, satisfied it'd be a better choice than the dense cluster of molten planets they passed through. As they fell into orbit at a reasonable distance from the planet, she engaged the autopilot and reached for her mug of water.

"Cassia, why don't you scan the planet and see what we're looking at?" Dani stared at the blue surface, sprinkled with patches of what appeared to be water.

Dani relaxed, resting her head back on her headrest, and opened the solar shades to get a better view of the planet. She'd about had it with whatever the black, gelatinous organism was. She glanced down at her console and flipped through the status screens. Shields were holding at two percent, but the tracker orbs were gone.

"I sure hope you can figure out where we are, Cruz, because it might be a while before the *Houston* can track us down since we lost our orbs somewhere along the way." Dani waited for the ding of acknowledgement, but it didn't come. She looked up toward Cruz's station. He sat still, staring at his display. "Cruz?"

He slowly lifted his eyes and pressed his lips together, furrowing his brow. His eyes caught Dani's. The confusion splayed across his face caused a feeling of dread to wash over her. Cruz was the most reliable navigator she had ever met, and he had never failed to pinpoint their location before. But this time, the bewildered look on his face made her extremely uncomfortable.

"We're in uncharted territory," he signed, confirming her fear.

CHAPTER 5

Dani stood next to Cruz's seat, bending over the console with him as they ran yet another scan on the celestial bodies near and far and sighed heavily. "Not a single hit."

Cruz typically could figure out where they were based on the planets in the system itself. When that didn't work, he relied on the computer's system to map out their location in relation to key stars and planets around them while cross-referencing the GC database. Only this time, not even that technique was working.

Zadria peered over her shoulder. "I'm out of ideas, too. This is virtually impossible without a point of reference."

Dani stood and stretched her back. Only she, Cruz, Cassia, and Zadria remained in the bridge. Howard and Jag were looking over the ship's systems and engines. The past few hours had been spent running every scan possible to determine their location with no success. The monotony of it all was starting to wear on Dani and the crew.

She walked around to the holographic display of their current planetary system and ran a hand through her hair. "Okay, let's run through this again. The hop caused us to exit the wormhole prematurely. That leaves us without an entrance point to go back the way we came, which even if we could there's the matter of the organism."

Cruz joined Dani and zoomed out on the holographic display. *"We can't get a lock on our location. I've programmed the navigation system to try to take account of any possible points of reference, but we've got to be pretty far out of the charted areas to have this much difficulty pinpointing where we are."*

Dani nodded. "Okay, now let's go over what we have going for us."

Zadria looked up from her tablet. "We have enough supplies to last us several weeks."

"If needed, we could probably gather more supplies on the planet. Scans indicate a survivable atmosphere as well as water, so the planet is capable of supporting a variety of lifeforms," Cassia chimed in.

"Well." Howard entered the bridge, wiping his hands on a cloth clipped to his work-belt. "The good news is that Jag and I made a few adjustments to allow the ship to recharge a little faster."

Jag had entered just behind Howard and quickly made his way to his station. "Shields are now at nine percent and climbing. The jump drive is charging as well, though more slowly."

"Good work, guys. Cassia, what else do you know about the planet?" Dani asked as she made her way to Cassia's station.

"Well, I know you're going to want to see this." Cassia leaned to the side to allow Dani a better view.

Dani leaned in and scrolled through the scan details. "Oh, wow. Put it up on half of the main screen."

Cassia displayed the scan details. The atmosphere was oxygen-rich so they'd have no problems breathing should they need to land. There were also several bodies of water dappling the sphere. The planet itself seemed to lack large oceans; however, the many sizable lakes covered roughly fifty-five percent of the surface. Mountain ranges crested like winding snakes across the globe, dividing the land into what appeared to be different habitats.

A list of resources scrolled across the images of the planet, causing Zadria's eyes to widen. "Twenty-eight percent of the planet is covered in glowshard. That's the highest percentage I've ever seen. This is a huge find! If other planets in this system are like this then the GC will want to establish colonies here as soon as possible."

"Huh." Howard's fingers ran down the list on the main screen. "Interesting."

Dani perked an eyebrow. "What is it?"

"Lots of good stuff down there. Especially this." His finger landed and tapped about halfway down the list.

"Egniorium, isn't that what they use to power hyperdrive technology?" Jag asked from his station.

Howard nodded. "It is. In fact, depending on the quality of it, I might be able to convert the jump drive to a hyperdrive, at least temporarily."

Dani smiled. "Well, that's something. How much do you need?"

"I'll run some calculations and let you know." Howard scratched his chin. "I don't know how much good it will do us if we can't figure out which direction to go, though."

"Let us worry about that." Dani made her way back to Cruz's station. "You find out what we need. Jag, go prep the cruiser for a trip down to the planet."

"You got it," Jag said as he left the bridge.

"Cruz, can you program a search based on our origin and set it to reevaluate at periodic intervals? Maybe we can figure out our last known location and work from there."

"*You bet*," Cruz signed before getting to work whipping through the screens on his console.

"Hey Dani." Cassia's voice wavered slightly. "Can you come here for a minute?"

Concerned, Dani crossed the bridge to Cassia's station. "What's up?"

"I'm running a more detailed scan of the surface. There don't appear to be any signs of civilization."

"Good. We won't have to worry about negotiating then." Dani shrugged.

"But look at this." Cassia pointed to her central display. "These marks here are lifeforms, reptilian it seems. Their behavior and brain-to-mass ratio indicates they're also rather primitive."

"They're big," Dani observed, starting to understand Cassia's nervousness.

"Just wait," Cassia said as she stroked Carl, who was purring in her lap.

Dani stared intently at the screen, narrowing her eyes. Five large lifeforms slowly circled a smaller creature. Dani pressed her lips together and took a deep breath, holding it. She could already guess where this was going.

Cassia and Dani both jumped slightly as the five larger lifeforms suddenly converged on the smaller one.

Dani clamped a hand over her mouth. "They're fast," she mumbled through her fingers.

Cassia nodded, looking distressed.

Dani stood and bit her lip, looking around the bridge. What she thought would be a two-man job was starting to look more like she'd need a small army. Her eyes landed on Cruz across the bridge. His military ground experience would certainly help them out. "Cruz, can you come over here please?"

Cruz looked up from his screen for a moment before leaning back down, hitting a few keys, then making his way across the bridge. Dani couldn't help but notice the spring in his step that he'd regained with the new prosthetics. Even though working with Patrick could be difficult at times, it wasn't without its perks.

"Cassia, show him," Dani ordered.

Cruz watched with a trained eye, not flinching as the hunting pack picked off another smaller creature.

Dani waited until Cruz looked up from the screen and caught her eye. She was relieved that there wasn't an ounce of fear in his expression.

"*We're going to need a lot of ammo,*" he signed. "*I'll go check the armory.*"

Dani nodded to Cruz and he left the bridge.

"Dani?" Cassia muttered quietly.

"Yeah?" She turned to her crewmate, her friend. Cassia's eyes were the opposites of Cruz's. Instead of a distinct lack of fear, hers were brimming with it.

"Be careful."

Dani patted Cassia on the shoulder and attempted a reassuring smile before walking over to Howard. "Looks like it could get ugly down there."

Howard looked up from his calculations. His vantage point would have allowed him to watch Cassia's screens as they examined the lifeforms. "I wish there were another way, but I am coming up dry."

"Did you figure out how much of this stuff we'll need?"

"More or less. I still need to work out a few details but if you can bring back around fifteen pounds, that should do the trick with a little leftover."

"Oh, well that doesn't seem too bad," Dani mused. "How's everything else looking?"

"Shields are at sixty-two percent, jump drive is just over forty."

"Good." Dani blew out a deep breath and gestured to Cassia's station. "So, I take it you saw?"

Howard nodded slowly but didn't say anything. He didn't need to; his feelings on the matter were written all over his face in deep lines of worry.

"I'll put Z in charge while we're down there so you can focus on making the adjustments to the jump drive."

"Sounds good. Good luck, Dani."

"Hey, Z. You're in charge. Take good care of the ship. We'll be back as soon as we can."

"Yes, Captain." Zadria stood and saluted.

Dani returned the gesture a bit uncomfortably, as she wasn't used to saluting in the comfort of her own ship, but she didn't feel as though now was the appropriate time to come down on the girl. Dani herself remembered her rookie day, fresh out of the academy at the young age of twenty-one. She, too, was eager to please—and possibly annoyingly so.

Dani turned and nodded to Cassia, who she thought might rub the fur off the cat with as quickly as her hand ran down the length of his back, but Carl didn't seem to mind.

She left the bridge and made her way down to the cruiser. Jag and Cruz were already geared up in protective armor and checking their weapons. Cruz passed Dani a reinforced armor suit, and Jag pulled another rifle and two more handguns from the weapons closet.

"I trust Cruz informed you of the situation?" she asked Jag as she got into her gear and tied her hair back.

"Yup, sounds like we're going to want to get in and out of there as quick as possible."

Dani nodded. "Howard says we only need about fifteen pounds of this stuff, so hopefully we can find it all in one place."

The three of them climbed into the cruiser, Jag taking the pilot seat and Dani taking the co-pilot seat next to him while Cruz clipped their weapons into the secure holder and placed a case marked 'explosives' in the cargo area.

"Alright, Cassia, can you hear us?" Dani spoke into her comm.

"Loud and clear," Cassia replied. "I ran a scan and found a large egniorium deposit. It's nestled between several lakes and appears relatively isolated from the hunting plains where we saw the predatory creatures. Unfortunately, you can't land on the doorstep so it will be a bit of a hike. I'll send Jag the coordinates now."

"Sounds good. Got the coordinates, disengaging from *Osirion* now."

The cruiser released from *Osirion*'s belly and maneuvered in the direction of the violet planet below. As they drew closer, the purple, silver, and blue cloud cover obscured much of the green-blue foliage below, but not completely. Dani raised the shields on the cruiser to prepare for reentry as Jag guided the small craft toward the planet's surface. They dove through the thick clouds and into the crisp air below.

"Sensors confirm that the air is oxygen rich. Shouldn't have any problem breathing here," Dani reported, happy to see that their original scans were accurate.

The canopy of blue-tinted leaves covered this area of the planet, only breaking away for the occasional clearing. Small featherless flying creatures, remarkably similar to bats with beaks, left the protection of the trees below to swarm around the cruiser.

"Ugly little guys." Jag wrinkled his nose as he glanced out the window at one of the pointy-nosed, splotchy-skinned fliers.

Not long after, a much larger flying creature took to the air. The tree it launched from shook considerably as the winged beast became airborne. Tufts of scraggly yellow and red feathers ruffled as the creature shrieked and snatched two pawfuls of the smaller lifeform before practically crashing back into the canopy, sending a slew of more featherless bird-like animals into the air.

A second unkempt, winged beast propelled from the canopy, this time toward the cruiser. It soared up near the windshield, bits of flesh dangling from its fanged mouth. It screeched, the remnants from its previous meal falling to the earth below.

"Gross," Jag mumbled as he split his attention between the creature and the looming mountain ridge ahead.

The rocky peaks seemed to be relatively innocuous at first glance. But as they drew nearer, the crew could see thick coils writhing around the peaks.

"Pull up, Jag," Dani ordered as she eyed the shifting ground cautiously. Aside from the large beast flying alongside them, the rest of the flying wildlife had remained over the lush canopy. Dani wasn't sure if their absence here was due to the lack of foliage or something else, but she didn't want to take any chances.

Jag complied and the cruiser climbed in altitude. The beast screeched once more and accelerated ahead of the cruiser.

As they reached the summits, Dani could see that the writhing ground wasn't ground at all but a nest of massive snake-like creatures. Claws along their tails clamped down on the stone as the snakes launched their heads toward the cruiser with snapping jaws, the claws anchoring them from leaving the safety of the cliffs. Thankfully, the cruiser was out of reach, but the flying predator was not.

The first snake made purchase with the animal's fleshy belly, causing it to jerk in the air and immediately circle around due to the tether created by the snake. Within a few seconds, more snakes sank their fangs into the massive beast and pulled it down to their roost. The screeches instantly went from a sound of aggression to one of pain.

Dani, Cruz, and Jag exchanged glances as the shrieking stopped.

"Good call," Jag said, his knuckles white as he held onto the yoke.

"Looks like the egniorium deposit is in this valley." Dani checked Cassia's coordinates with their current location. "Let's see if we can find a good place to land."

"*I suggest staying away from the hunting fields*," Cruz signed before pointing to a large swath of land covered in tall, bluish grasses and squat, green trees.

Dani nodded. "Agreed. With what we've seen on this planet so far, I don't want to mess with any of the predators around here. They mean business."

"Coming up on a landing site." Jag flipped a switch to drop the landing gear and another to power on the landing thrusters.

The tall grass and shrubs below stirred, causing Dani to shift uncomfortably. Her suspicions were confirmed as a thick, scaly tail rose from the grass momentarily before running in the direction they were flying.

"We've got company," Dani alerted Cruz and Jag.

They continued drop in altitude, the creature that moved through the grass keeping pace with the ship.

"There's a few over here, too." Jag nodded out his side of the cruiser.

Dani frowned, watching three more swaths of grass rustling alongside the ship's path.

The lakes passed by below them as Jag made his way toward a flat area of ground. The creatures halted just before the grass's edge as the cruiser glided over the mirrored lake surfaces, causing ripples to fan out on each one. Once across, Jag carefully lowered the cruiser, small trees and grass swaying from the landing thrusters. "*Osirion,* we've landed. Stand by."

The network of lakes lay just ahead with a glowshard-covered hill at their center. The exterior of the hill was the same sponge-like, blue-green-purple material that made up the exterior of *Osirion.* It comprised millions of tiny organisms all working together to form a tough, self-healing skin. The glowshard was able to live in nearly any environment, but it did require specific conditions for its self-healing properties.

Dani, Jag, and Cruz leapt into action as soon as the thrusters shut down. They quickly donned their helmets and holstered their handguns, picking up the rifles last.

"Cassia, do you read?"

"Yes, Dani, I'm here."

"How's it looking out there?"

"I'm not seeing anything in your immediate vicinity. The lifeforms seem to have returned to the prairie. The scans show me that you landed near the egniorium deposit. It's just there at the center of the lakes."

"Looks like there's a cave right there along the water's edge." Jag pointed out the window.

"Alright, Jag." Dani grabbed two port-cons from their docking stations on the cruiser and powered them up. "I need you to go in and get the egniorium, fifteen pounds of it. Cruz and I will watch your back. I don't know if this will work in there, but take it anyway."

A honeycomb structure of smaller lakes lay before them. Land bridges no more than a few feet wide divided the lakes and ultimately led to the hill at the center.

Dani stepped out of the cruiser, squinting as the sun glinted off of the settling water.

"Looks like we'll have to wind our way over there."

Cruz and Jag joined her, carrying the supplies. Expanding out from the lakes was a variety of landscapes. A mountain range began its upward slope behind them. To the left and right were the prairie hunting lands for the unnaturally quick predators. And directly ahead, beyond the lakes, lay a grove of the low, wide trees.

Dani passed the first port-con to Jag and adjusted the second, attaching it to her left forearm. "These won't be effective for sensing lifeforms more than a few yards away, so we're relying on Cassia's eye in the sky."

"You got it," Cassia replied. "Z has us locking in orbit above you, so I'm watching. So far the big ones are still on the other side of the lake."

"Egniorium is pretty soft," Howard chimed in. "It's red and should look kind of like cloudy gelatin. Don't let its appearance fool you, though. Despite its malleability, it's quite heavy. Oh, and don't shoot at it or blow it up because you'll die."

Jag snorted and grinned. "You almost left that little detail out, didn't you, old man?"

"I told ya, didn't I?" Howard's chuckle rang out across the comm.

"Let's get a move on," Dani said as she started toward the first path of land running between two lakes. She would have loved to take more time to enjoy the beauty of the planet. It wasn't often that she had the opportunity to explore on this level. However, the constant stirring of the tall grass from the gentle breeze made Dani uneasy, especially after witnessing how quickly the predators moved.

Dani kept a watchful eye as she navigated them along the network of glowshard-covered stone paths toward the center. The occasional glance down allowed her to see deep into the pools of water surrounding them. Vibrant green fish darted away from the trio and down into the deep blue as they passed.

Dani turned when she reached the cave to look out across the land again. "Cassia, you're sure there aren't any signs of civilization? I don't want to be stealing someone's egniorium. I know how valuable it is."

"No, scans didn't pick up any tech readings or find any indications of civilization. If someone is here, they've done a really great job of hiding themselves."

"Hey, Howie, there's some of this red stuff on the ground here outside the cave." Jag knelt down to examine some faded red crystals.

"That's no good to us. We need stone that hasn't been exposed to the sun's rays. It weakens it, making it brittle and useless."

"Gotcha." Jag sighed. He picked up one of the red stones and crushed it easily between his fingers.

Dani proceeded to the mouth of the cave, turning on the light mounted on her rifle and shining it into the entrance. The cave was small, but it was large enough that the sun didn't seem to reach the back half of the cave. She squinted at the dim glow produced by the light on her rifle, but couldn't tell for sure if any of the egniorium that showed up on the scans was easily accessible.

"Looks good, Jag. Get in there and get us what we need. Cruz and I will wait here. Stay on comms."

Jag made his way into the cave, sweeping his lit weapon to and fro.

Dani turned to face Cruz, who was perched on a rock and staring across the network of lakes through his scope. Dani followed his gaze to the tall grass on the other side. Several tails, she counted seven, waved in the air in a circle. Dani whispered, "Looks like they caught something."

Cruz remained motionless, staring at the herd while Dani slowly scanned the area around the lakes once more. Movement near the ship caught her eye, and she crouched down, lifting her rifle and taking aim.

Though Dani's father spent much of his time away on missions, they did bond over some common hobbies, one of them being hunting. Bob Devereaux was a sportsman at heart, though he wasn't one who only hunted for the trophy. He prided himself on always having a fair hunt and using as much of his prey as possible. There was a calm about him when they were on their excursions. He always told Dani that there was something so centering about being out in the wilderness.

As Dani peered through her scope, she could make a slight outline of a smaller animal at the edge of the grass. She wasn't able to tell exactly what it was, but she knew it was there. She pulled her eyes away for the briefest of seconds to glance at her port-con and make sure no other, larger lifeforms were closing in.

She took a deep breath, everything seeming so clear. Each blade of grass was in focus. The gentle breeze across her cheek shifted, placing them upwind of the small animal. The movement stopped.

Dani held perfectly still, waiting. Patience was key in a hunt, but despite her experience, she didn't want to shoot the creature if she didn't have to. Dani whispered into the comm, "How's it going in there, Jag?"

"Found a nice sized deposit and I'm working on carving the egniorium out now," his hushed reply returned.

A short, quiet whistle came from Cruz's direction.

Dani lifted her eyes to his perch, keeping her weapon trained in the direction of the creature.

"*They're moving around the lakes,*" he signed, then pointed.

The creatures cut paths through the tall grass alongside the water, working their way along the outer edge of the lake area and back toward the cruiser. An occasional glimpse of thick, scaled tail was their only identifying trait.

The grass rustled, and a quiet sound emerged from the shrubbery, something between a chirp and a mew. Dani's eyes flew to the source of the noise as it stepped into a small opening. Her heart started to race as the medium-sized creature spotted her. Its face was long and flat with pointed teeth angling out of its jaw. It stood on its back two muscular legs while one of its front claws clutched a small, wriggling, furry creature. The other arm steadied the mix of what Dani could only describe as a crocodile and gorilla, the likes of which she had never seen before.

Dark scales and tufts of either fur or fine feathers coated its body. But the characteristic Dani couldn't take her eyes off of was the tail, a smaller version of the tails belonging to the creatures making their way around the lake.

She had seen the dark tufts of fur-like feathers all around the entrance of the cave, but she'd assumed they belonged to some kind of bird. It didn't take her long after spotting the creature to realize she was woefully wrong.

"We have a problem," she whispered, sitting motionless as the realization came to her. "I think we're in their nest."

As soon as Dani finished talking, the creature before her dropped the animal it held, which scampered into the undergrowth. It crouched down, facing her, much like Carl would just before he pounced on whatever he was stalking at the time. She was unsure if it wanted to play or was getting ready to attack; regardless, she switched the safety off on her weapon.

Then the creature shrieked the most awful scream Dani had ever heard.

.

CHAPTER 6

T he noise from the animal stopped Dani's heart as her eyes darted to the far end of the lakes that the creatures were rounding. Their movement stopped, but only for the briefest of seconds. A moment later, they were on a full-on run toward the cruiser and what Dani guessed to be their young.

"Lifeforms coming in fast!" Cassia called out through the comm.

"Jag, grab what you can and get out of there," Dani ordered as she and Cruz hurried behind a large rock at the water's edge. They took aim where the tall grass ended as they watched the tails swarm closer. The youngling screeched again before sprinting toward them along the stone laced between the lakes and toward the cave.

Dani started to pivot toward the smaller animal when the rest of the herd erupted from the grass. A mess of muscle, snapping jaws, and deep-throated roars erupted from the mass of creatures. Dani turned back to them and opened fire along with Cruz, ignoring the smaller, less threatening version of the beast as it ran into the cave behind them.

"Jag, you've got company!" she shouted as she fired shot after shot into the herd.

The beasts stumbled but didn't stop. Their thick hides held up well against the ammunition, leaving only minor wounds that seeped with a vibrant purple ooze. The ineffective bullets seemed to anger the beasts as their roars increased in volume and intensity.

Rocks and dirt slid down the hillside beside Dani. She swung her weapon toward the origin of the disturbance and was surprised to see a leather-clad woman sliding gracefully down the side of the hill, bow drawn. The wind tousled the woman's vibrant red hair as she skidded to a stop at the bottom of the hill. She loosed a well-timed arrow straight into the open jaws of one of the beasts, the tip protruding through the back of the skull.

Dani's eyes widened as they met Cruz's and they imitated their sudden ally and aimed for the mouths of the beasts when they roared. One of Cruz's shots hit its target as it found its way into the gaping mouth of a large beast, blowing out through the back of its skull and dropping the now-lifeless animal to the ground. The others paused a moment to look at their fallen kin before roaring anew and resuming their charge.

They continued to fight alongside the redheaded woman as the creatures made their way through the maze of lakes and stone. Even the non-lethal hits were slowing them down, slightly. However, the remaining beasts seemed to grow stronger and more determined as each creature fell.

Another beast splashed into a pool alongside the path, its massive tail causing the next to fall in as well. However, the second animal quickly recovered and climbed out of the water to resume its charge.

"Gaaah!" Jag's scream echoed in Dani's head through the comm, followed by gunfire.

"Jag, you alright?" Dani shouted over the firefight.

"Let's just get the hell out of here!" he shouted again, running up beside her with a limp and taking aim along with Dani and Cruz after a momentary glance at the stranger.

Dani and Cruz's rifles ran out of ammunition and were tossed aside as the pair drew their handguns. The redheaded woman ran out of arrows and drew a long, curved blade from a sheath.

Another one down, three left, but they were too close. The guns slowed the pace of the herd significantly, but they weren't enough to stop it. Cruz holstered his weapon as the animals closed the remaining distance, and then he pulled a large knife from his utility belt.

With all the grace of a skilled fighter, Cruz launched himself over the rock and tackled the first creature, thrusting his knife into its mouth and out the top of its head. He quickly retracted his arm with a twist and charged the next beast while Dani and Jag shot at the third.

Uncharted Territory

A poorly timed roar resulted in the demise of the creature Jag and Dani shot at while the last menacing beast threw Cruz to the ground and lumbered over him.

Jag leapt on the animal's back, drawing his own knife and attempting to shove it into the creature's neck. The rough scales deflected the blade, causing only a shallow cut, but one deep enough to draw more of the purple ooze.

Angry, the beast reached back and pulled Jag off, throwing him at Dani before turning to Cruz once more with another loud roar. Cruz quickly drew his handgun and fired into the creature's mouth three times, causing it to stumble forward and fall on him.

The redheaded woman hurried to Cruz's side and tugged on the beast in a fruitless effort to free him.

Dani and Jag untangled themselves and scrambled to their feet. Jag's knife had slit across Dani's side between her armored plates during the collision, and she winced in pain as she straightened out her torso. The two hurried to Cruz's side and tried to roll the heavy beast off of him.

After several pulls and some pushing on Cruz's part, the four of them were finally able to remove the beast and free Cruz.

In the distance another roar sounded.

"Let's get the hell out of here!" Dani shouted as she ran toward the cruiser, holding her side.

Cruz quickly grabbed her by the wrist and pointed to another grouping of the dinosaur-like tails running toward the cruiser.

"The cruiser is surrounded. Head for the grove of trees if you can. I don't see any lifeforms that direction," Cassia called through the comm.

Dani turned to run the opposite direction, but she lost her footing on the purple ooze–covered stone and slipped down, into the water. Her equipment weighed her down, and the cut on her side stung fiercely at the exposure to the water, limiting her ability to quickly recover. She knew how to swim, but the water in the lake provided her with less buoyancy than she had ever experienced.

Her kicks and attempts to grab onto the side of the stone wall were futile as she rapidly sank deeper and deeper below the surface. In a desperate attempt to save herself, she started to unclip gear from her body, but before she could release her pack, a wave of red hair dove into the water beside her. The warrior woman hooked her arm under Dani's and kicked off the wall, back toward the surface, where Cruz quickly grabbed Dani by the armored plate on her chest and hoisted her out of the water.

Dani sputtered and gasped as the woman climbed out and grabbed Dani by the arm once more, practically dragging her along the path. Cruz followed close behind, glancing back over his shoulder at the cruiser, where the creatures had just emerged from the brush.

Jag was near the edge of the lake system, limping along with a pained look on his face. He stopped and stared back at Dani and the others. "Is she okay?"

"Go!" Dani yelled and waved at him between coughs as she struggled to keep up with the red-haired woman. Her lungs burned, but stopping wasn't an option at this point.

The woman reached Jag and grabbed the egniorium bag from his hands. He started to protest, but more frantic waves from Dani convinced him to let it go. The warrior woman swung the bag up over her shoulder and set off in a dead sprint toward the trees.

Dani was impressed with the woman's speed and thankful for her help. Without the extra weight, Jag was getting along a little better, but Dani and Cruz still caught up with him rather quickly, and if they could, the beasts could.

She glanced back across the honeycomb of stone and water and saw the creatures were quickly gaining ground and were nearly to the cave. Had it been open field, they would have surely been dead by now. Dani swung around to look toward the trees. They seemed so close, yet so far away.

"Cruz, get Jag," Dani ordered as she firmly placed her hand on her side and tried to pick up the pace.

In near effortlessness, Cruz bent and angled his shoulder under Jag's arm on the side of Jag's injured leg and grabbed him around the back. His muscles flexed as he started to run, Jag bouncing along beside him on his good leg. They made quick time and caught up to Dani with relative ease. She gritted her teeth and tried to ignore the pain as they made their way toward the thick trees.

The warrior woman reappeared through the foliage and waved them closer, but as they neared she held up her hands, gesturing for them to stop. The trio quickly came to a halt and saw the reason for the woman's hesitation. The trees were covered with gigantic thorns as big as Dani's forearm. At the end of each glistened a drop of amber-colored liquid, sparkling in the sunlight.

The woman beckoned for them to follow her and carefully stepped between a pair of the trees that were slightly more spaced out that the rest. Dani followed next, contorting her body away from the dagger-like thorns and into the darkness of the grove. Once she reached an area where she could turn around, she helped guide Jag through, then Cruz.

Within the safety of trees, Dani and her crew could hear the animals shrieking, but they didn't follow. Even without the thorns, the trees were much too close for the large beasts to find their way through, and Dani felt relief for the first time since the youngling first appeared.

"I think we're safe." She sighed. "Cassia, do you have eyes on us?"

"Yeah, but the animals are circling the grove so you probably should stay put for a while."

"Well, we can't exactly stop here. There's not even room to sit, let alone do anything else," Jag complained as he tried to find a safe spot on a nearby tree to lean on.

"*Where'd that woman go?*" Cruz signed, peering through the trees around them. "*She seems like she knows the way.*"

Dani rotated in the small area before spotting the woman's red hair through the mess of trunks and thorns. "This way."

They continued on, following the mysterious warrior woman as the trees grew even denser and the light filtering through the leaves overhead grew dim. Finally, they stumbled into an opening in the foliage. The break in the trees was smaller than the cruiser but had enough room for them to stretch and rest without the fear of being impaled.

Uncharted Territory

At the center of a clearing was a circle of stones with charred wood in the center. The egniorium bag lay next to the fire pit. Cruz walked over and scooped up the bag, placing it in the shade at the edge of the grove.

The red-haired woman was kneeling below a torn canopy of lightweight fabric. Ropes secured the fabric to trees, and the trees beneath the awning had been dethorned. Dani wrinkled her forehead as she took in the rest of the camp. The grass in the clearing was packed down and looked like it had been for some time. The areas on the trees where the thorns had been removed seemed to be healed over. Under the canopy lay a bed of leaves and grass along with a stack of firewood.

"Hey," Dani said quietly as she approached the woman. "Thank you."

The woman turned and smiled at Dani before handing her a length of rope tied to a tarp and pointing to a tree on the opposite side of the clearing. Dani followed her instructions, securing the tarp as the woman ran around and secured the other three corners. She looked up at the darkening sky then gestured for Dani and her crew to climb beneath the tarp.

"Have you been here long?" Dani asked, signing as she spoke in hopes the woman would be able to understand her. Instead, she just received a blank stare.

"It's sure be nice to have Cassia around right now. She knows more languages than anyone I know," Jag said as he examined his leg. "Of course, I don't think she would have made it through all of that without having a breakdown."

Cruz swung his hand back and thumped Jag in the chest with a glare.

"Ow! Geez, beat up the injured guy. You know it's true though."

"I can hear you." Cassia sounded annoyed over the comm.

Jag's eyes widened. "Er, sorry, but these things were crazy."

"It's fine, I don't want to be down there either. But tell me about the person that you're with. Maybe I can help you communicate with her."

"I'm not so sure she's a person actually, but humanoid for sure." Jag cocked his head to the side as he stared at the woman, who

116

was carving the meat off of something she dug out of the fire pit.

Dani followed his gaze and started to notice subtle differences in the woman that she hadn't seen clearly before. What she thought was armor in the heat of battle was actually the woman's skin. Scales covered her exposed forearms and lower legs. They also framed the outside of her face along her hairline but not around her features, still allowing for movement and expression.

"I'll amplify the comm signal so you can pick up anything she says," Dani said as she adjusted the dials on her comm device.

"*Ræmâ,*" the woman said as she presented bits of deep pink flesh to Dani, Cruz, and Jag on a flat stone.

"*I think that's dinner,*" Cruz signed before smiling, nodding, and taking a handful of the meat.

Dani did the same. "Thank you."

Jag stared at the meat before looking at Dani. "You know, I think I'll be fine."

"Eat it." Dani frowned at him. "You're injured. You need to eat."

Jag stretched out his leg with a grimace and examined it before giving the woman a half smile as he retrieved a bit of the meat. "Thanks."

"*Viniramâgi anćer da*?" she asked as she knelt next to Jag's leg and peered at the blood seeping from the wound at his knee. Without waiting for a response, she took out her large, curved knife and reached for his leg.

"Whoa!" Jag's eyes widened and he held up his hands in front of the wound. "It's just a bite, no reason to get crazy with that thing. Dani, do something."

Dani knelt next to the woman and peeled back a torn section of the blood-soaked clothing. "It looks pretty bad."

Cruz joined them. "*We need to stop the bleeding.*"

The woman looked between the three of them and then reached for Jag's leg again. With a quick swipe of the knife, she sheared the tattered clothing and armored plates away from his leg, just above the knee. The bite mark was distinct, with several puncture holes where half a dozen teeth had broken through the flesh. The skin around each puncture was starting to darken, and the blood seeping out was a deeper red than Dani had ever seen with an injury.

The woman stood and stepped out of the clearing, leaving the three of them alone. Cruz took his canteen and poured some water over the wound, causing Jag to wince. He opened his first-aid kit and took out some gauze and antibacterial ointment, but before he could apply any, the woman reappeared.

In her hands she held a large thorn from one of the trees, half full of the amber-like liquid. In the other hand she clutched a handful of small, white flowers. She knelt next to Jag once more, carefully passing the hollow, liquid-filled thorn to Cruz before meticulously pulling the petals off of each of the flowers and shoving them into her mouth. As she chewed on the petals, she rubbed the flowers' centers on Jag's wound, leaving a dusting of yellow.

"Oh, that feels nice." Jag smiled and relaxed his shoulders somewhat.

The red-haired woman took the thorn back from Cruz and spit the broken down petals inside. She swirled the concoction and plucked a palm-sized leaf from a nearby bush.

"She's not gonna..." Jag started, but before he could finish, she slathered the yellow-and-white-speckled salve first on the leaf, then on Jag's wound, eliciting a yelp from the patient. Jag cringed. "Yup, that just happened."

Dani watched the woman, who sat back and watched Jag's wound closely. She seemed to be aware of what she was doing—at least Dani hoped that she was.

Jag's face slowly morphed from a look of mild discomfort to one of overwhelming pain. "Gah! That *burns*! Stop her, Cruz!" he hollered.

"*She looks like she knows what she's doing,*" Cruz signed and sat back, watching her.

"Can I please have more of those flowers? They were nice. Took away the pain. Would love some more of that," Jag rambled through his clenched jaw.

The blood trickling from his wounds ceased, and the woman smiled and passed the thorn back to Cruz, who pushed it into the ground so it wouldn't topple.

"Thank you," Dani said, relieved. Jag had lost a fair amount of blood and she was happy that the woman's medicine had put a stop to it. "What can we call you?"

A confused look from the woman caused Dani to frown. She decided to try another approach and touched her own chest, then pointed to Jag and Cruz in turn. "Dani, Jag, Cruz."

The woman's eyes followed Dani's pointing and she nodded in understanding before tapping her own chest. "Sylvine."

"Sylvine," Dani repeated with a smile before pointing to Jag's wound. "Thank you."

Sylvine peered past Dani at the wound and retrieved more of the salve from within the thorn, slathering it on again.

"No, not necess—" Jag squeezed his eyes shut, then after Sylvine was finished, he slowly opened one. "Oh, it wasn't so bad that time."

A loud crack of thunder overhead pulled the group's attention to the black, billowy clouds rolling in overhead.

"*Kunshe,*" Sylvine said as she pointed to the sky. She quickly covered the firepit with a wide rock and retreated to her shelter just as the rain started to fall.

CHAPTER 7

L arge drops of water drummed on the tarp overhead as Dani stared at it. She lay on her back, nestled in the cramped space between Cruz and Jag with her hands folded on her stomach. Every few minutes, her attention shifted from the pooling water overhead to Jag. He lay silently with his eyes closed—that is, until her gaze lingered a little too long. Then he'd pop an eye open and she'd quickly look away. At times his breathing seemed labored and she worried about his injury, but he didn't seem to be in too much pain.

The cut on her side bothered her somewhat, but not enough to bring to anyone's attention. She didn't want to waste any medical supplies on her minor wound when Jag's seemed so much worse.

The water pooled in the center of the tarp until a stream formed, running from the top. Sylvine jumped up and gathered the rainwater in a large bottle and drank from it before offering it to the Dani, Cruz, and Jag.

Dani, propping herself up, welcomed the offer. The crisp water was delicious and helped Dani clear her mind. The storm had been raging for about an hour, but the lightning and thunder were starting to die down. "Cassia, can you give me an update on those beasts?"

"Wha? Oh, yeah, sure. One sec." Cassia yawned. "I'm not seeing any lifeforms in the prairie or near the lakes. There are a lot at the base of the mountains, but it looks like you should be able to get to the cruiser just fine."

"I think we should get going." Dani rolled off of her back and into a crouched position below the tarp. "Jag, are you okay to walk?"

"I think so." Jag grunted as he climbed to his feet, then immediately toppled into Dani. "Or not."

"Easy there." Dani laughed.

"Hey, you try getting up with a completely numb leg. Not so easy."

Cruz stood, grabbed the egniorium, and sturdied Jag while Dani gathered the rest of their belongings.

Sylvine popped up from her nest, looking alarmed. *"Ladonulkoshumnakir thaji. Ulchânma koshum kunshe."*

Dani took another look around the camp. Her eyes were drawn to the harness attached to the canopy over Sylvine's area. It was a parachute. Maybe Sylvine wasn't from this planet. It would make sense that she wasn't, since Cassia had found no signs of civilization. Dani gestured to Sylvine. "Sylvine, would you like to come with us?"

Sylvine watched Dani and the others as they prepared themselves to lead, the expression on her face a mix of worry and annoyance. Then, as the group stepped out from under the tarp and made their way over to the entrance into the clearing, she finally got up and hurriedly grabbed a satchel before joining them.

Dani led the way through the twisted trunks and thorns, helping guide Jag through while Cruz helped him from behind. Sylvine brought up the rear, collecting more

125

of the white flowers as well as thorns and strips of bark from here and there.

The rain was barely noticeable beneath the intertwined canopy of leaves, but the occasional roar of thunder and flash of lightning were still startling, even at several miles away. Despite the storm, the prairie was relatively well lit. The two moons peeked over the mountain ridge and lit up the area through a break in the clouds. Dani glanced skyward. "Are you still there, Cassia?"

"No, it's Zadria. Cassia really needed a break so I took over."

"Hey, Z. Good looking out. How are things looking out there? Anything I need to be aware of?"

"Doesn't look like it. Everything must be taking shelter in the storm, because the only things lighting up the sensors between you and the cruiser are the fish in the lakes."

"Great." The tension in Dani's neck eased slightly. "I can handle fish."

"Alright, guys, let's see if we can't get back to the cruiser and get off this planet." Dani stepped out and into the rain. The heavy drops quickly wetted and chilled her hair, then ran down her face. She knew that running around in a storm may not be the best idea, but she figured they might as well take advantage of the empty prairie while they could.

The group plodded along across the field, back toward the lakes and the cruiser. Dani continuously surveyed the surrounding area for any sign of the creatures. Their path was quiet, and wet. But they reached the lakes safely.

"Maybe we should go around," Dani said softly. "I don't know if anything's home in that cave and I really don't want to deal with those creatures again."

Lightning cracked across the sky above them and shot into the earth near the grove of trees where the once sought shelter. Another bolt burst from nearly the same area, crackling and charring the ground near the lakes.

"*Fænulkuzinakir thaji,*" Sylvine said from behind as she went around Dani and her crew and took the lead, working her way quietly and carefully across the network of land bridges.

"I don't know what she said, but I'm with her." Jag limped after Sylvine. "There's no way I'm getting hit by lighting on top of the chunk that thing took out of my leg."

Cruz simply nodded to Dani and followed the others, leaving Dani alone on the shore.

With a sigh, Dani shot a nervous glance toward the cave once more before she followed along, bringing up the rear of the line. She didn't like the thought of getting close to the creatures' den again, but she didn't like the idea of getting struck by lightning either. And it seemed that the storm was picking up again, illustrated by two more violent outbursts of lightning behind them.

Sylvine led the group on a different path than before, taking them around the den but still a shorter distance than they would have traveled had they avoided the lake network completely. Occasionally she'd stop and peer down into the water a moment before continuing. Dani wasn't sure if she was worried about her footing, or something else. But she made a mental note to have Cassia work with the woman to learn her language so they'd be able to communicate on a better level.

Uncharted Territory

Sylvine waved Cruz and Jag past her at an intersection of stone pathways and pointed to the cruiser before turning and walking toward the fallen beasts they'd slain earlier in the day. Dani stopped and watched her curiously as Cruz helped Jag to the cruiser.

Sylvine pulled a smaller pouch from the one she wore around her waist. She knelt next to one of the beasts and cut the tongue from its mouth and placed it in the bag before turning to repeat the process with the next fallen creature.

Dani was intrigued with her actions, but became distracted when the lake next to her began to release copious amounts of bubbles. She cocked her head, peering into the depths.

"*Degamkirit!*" Sylvine shouted as she pointed at the cruiser, clutching her bag of tongues.

Dani looked toward Cruz and Jag, thinking maybe they were in danger, but they were loading up without any apparent threat.

The bubbles started rising out of another nearby lake, and Dani watched them nervously, taking a quiet step toward the cruiser. Suddenly, she felt Sylvine's hand upon her wrist as the woman jerked her, nearly pulling her off her feet.

A series of roars and shrieks from the cave at the center of the lakes quickly caught Dani's attention. The creatures were awake—and they were mad.

"Shit," Dani mumbled as she tried to keep up with Sylvine on the slippery path.

Cruz was standing at the cruiser's hatch, raising his weapon and taking aim past the women.

Dani pulled Sylvine into a crouched position as they continued to hurry along, using her other hand for balance. Near the edge, Sylvine let go of Dani and turned, drawing her blade and dropping the bag of tongues into her pouch. Dani stumbled past her, then turned to look at the oncoming charge of beasts.

The thick-bodied, lizard-like beasts gathered at the opening of the cave, beating on their chests and on the ground. A few of the larger animals were making their way toward Dani and her crew, but they lacked the speed they'd had earlier in the day. Dani hurried and ducked into the cruiser with Sylvine and Cruz close behind, Cruz locking the hatch. Jag was already firing up the thrusters and preparing the cruiser for takeoff.

"Are you sure you can fly this thing right now? The storm is getting worse again." Dani watched as the lightning cracked across the sky over and over. She had tried to tune it out as she crossed the lake, but it had steadily been growing more frequent by the minute.

"We're about to find out!" Jag shouted back over the noise of the storm.

Cruz tapped Dani on the shoulder frantically, and pointed out the windshield toward the lake. The creatures had stopped in their tracks. Their attention was no longer locked on Dani and her crew, but instead on the bubbling water around them. Dani squinted through the rain-streaked windshield as Jag continued to run through the pre-flight checks.

Suddenly, a tentacle several times the length of the cruiser shot out of the water and fell across onto one of the creatures. It quickly coiled around the beast, which fruitlessly tried to scramble away, and pulled it down into the bubbling water.

"Holy cow," Jag shouted, "let's get out of here!"

He grabbed the yoke of the cruiser just as another tentacle, bigger than the first, erupted from the lake closest to them and dropped over the top of the cruiser.

"Get us out of here!" Dani ordered Jag.

"I can't get off the ground. That thing's too heavy." The cruiser's engines strained and the spacecraft lurched slightly, causing the tentacle to coil around them.

Dani's heart was in her chest. The cruiser was too large to get pulled down into one of the small pools, but she was still worried the creature would damage the ship.

Before she could think of a solution, Sylvine had thrown open the hatch and was hanging halfway out of the cruiser. With her long blade in hand and a swift downward motion, she severed the tentacle and swung the hatch shut once more.

"*Dekoshum!*" she shouted at Jag.

"Don't need a translator to tell me what that means," he quipped as the cruiser shuddered and rose off the ground. Jag gently rocked the small ship until the remaining length of tentacle slid off to the ground. From there, they quickly gained altitude and Jag flew toward the break in the clouds over the mountains. "Get strapped in. We're going to be leaving the atmosphere."

Dani, and Cruz quickly fastened their safety harnesses, then Sylvine did the same.

"Glad to hear you guys are on your way back," Zadria said over the comms. "We were a little worried there."

"You, missy, need to take another lesson on reading life signs. There was a little more than fish in those lakes." Jag laughed.

"Yeah, sorry," Zadria mumbled back. Dani could almost hear the embarrassment in her voice.

"Just have some medical supplies ready when we get there. Cruz and this lady did an alright patch job, but I wouldn't mind trading the spit for some actual bandages."

"Uh, okay," Zadria responded after a brief hesitation.

"Dani, I'm not feeling so great. Can you take over?" Jag asked.

She turned to him, noticing that much of the color had left his face, and quickly switched the controls over to her console. "You gonna be alright?"

"Oh, sure." Jag closed his eyes and leaned back in his seat. "I'll get patched up back on *Osirion* and be good as new."

Dani nodded, but bit the inside of her cheek, trying not to let the worry show. She was thankful the small craft piloted almost exactly like other GC spacecraft. It was easy flying back to *Osirion*. At one point, she carefully reached down to reassess the damage to her side. It felt like the wound had ripped open again in the commotion, but it didn't appear to be much worse.

On their approach to *Osirion*, she continued to glance at Jag to assess his state. Tiny beads of sweat were beginning to form on his forehead.

"Hanging in there, Jag?" she asked as she began the docking procedure.

He responded with a simple grunt.

As soon as the cruiser was locked in, Dani, Sylvine, and Cruz got up to help Jag through the hatch. The rest of the crew waited in the unloading area. They all paused to stare at the redheaded woman as she stepped out of the cruiser and took in her surroundings.

"Introductions later, people." Dani clapped her hands together, causing the crew to burst into action. Cassia passed Cruz the medical supplies, and Zadria offered water to each of them. Howard climbed into the cruiser and retrieved the egniorium.

"I'm going to get to work refining this. Shouldn't take too long, but I want to get us headed back as soon as possible." Howard stared at Jag's wound as he spoke; once more, the blood had started seeping out of several holes where the creature's teeth had pierced his flesh.

Cruz quickly wrapped Jag's wound and helped him to his feet. *"I'm not sure how long that will hold. We might need more of Sylvine's medicine to stop the bleeding again."*

"Oh, I don't think that's necessary, guys," Jag said as he stepped forward, crumpling into Dani and slowly sinking toward the ground in pain.

Dani did her best to hold him up. "You sure about that?"

"Well, maybe it's not such a bad idea," Jag grunted as Cruz hooked Jag's arm over his shoulders.

Dani frowned at Jag. He looked to be failing fast and hung limply from Cruz's shoulder. "We need to get him into bed."

Cruz nodded and scooped Jag up over his shoulder despite Jag's grunts of protest. Cruz began the climb up to the main level with Zadria in tow.

"Cassia, this is Sylvine. Please get her a translation chip."

"Already thought of that." Cassia smiled and placed the translation chip on Sylvine's lapel. "Although, I don't believe her language is in our database. The few words I picked up over the comm didn't have any hits on my translation software. I'll probably have to program her language in manually."

"Great. Get started on that as soon as you can. But first, I'd like to take her to Jag's room to see if she can do anything to help him like she did on the planet."

Cassia led the way up to the main level with Sylvine behind. Dani started up the ladder, but as she climbed, she was overcome with horrible nausea. She continued up the ladder and attempted to push the feeling aside, but it only grew in intensity, bringing lightheadedness with it. She stopped and hooked her arms around the ladder, squeezing her eyes shut in an effort to stop the ship from spinning and swaying around her, but to no avail.

Dani's grip failed and she felt herself falling toward the metal walkway below. Her head collided with the interior wall, and pain shot through her skull and down her neck. She looked up at Cassia and Sylvine peering down the ladder at her and tried to reach her hand toward them, but lacked the strength. Darkness started creeping in from the edges of her vision, spreading until it was all she could see, and she found herself floating in space once more.

CHAPTER 8

I t didn't take long for Dani to pinpoint her location as she floated through space. The star system that she fell into was as familiar to her as her childhood home. She was at the same coordinates that kept haunting her: the place where her father was killed.

Her consciousness seemed suspended without her body, the same way it had been when she'd experienced the execution at the prison. *Oh man, am I dead?* Dani willed herself to move and managed to float through the night sky, only this time something was different. There was a new planet in the system, and it bore an uncanny resemblance to the same blue planet they'd just visited.

Dani tried to put a stop to her drifting, but no amount of thought could contend with her momentum. The planet was coming, and it was coming fast. She braced herself for impact, but instead of feeling her body slam into the earth below, she merely stopped falling as soon as she neared the ground. The tall grass around her moved as though there was wind, but Dani felt none. She didn't seem to exist in any special form that she could imagine; instead, she seemed to just be a floating consciousness.

"Hey, kiddo, ready to head out?" Dani's father stepped out of the brush and approached her, rifle slung over his shoulder, hand extended.

Dani caught a glimpse of her adolescent self in his sunglasses and looked down at her hands before reaching to take his. The warm, rough grip of her father's hand was incredibly reassuring and familiar as he led her back into the brush.

"The beasts are ahead; they just got a kill and are feeding. We should be able to limit their numbers," Dani's father explained as though nothing had ever happened.

Dani stared at him in awe, knowing this had to be a dream. There was no way he could be here right now, unless she was dead after all.

Uncharted Territory

The pair stopped, and her father parted the grass to show a ring of the beasts hunched over, pushing raw flesh into their maws with their hands, tails in the air for balance. That was when Dani noticed the prey. The floral dress being trampled beneath their feet was her mother's favorite.

"Dad," Dani gasped, grabbing onto his arm. "They've got Mom."

Suddenly, her dad's arm wasn't his arm at all, but instead the branch of a lifeless tree. The bark crumbled away at her touch.

"Dad?" Dani questioned as she stepped back from the tree slowly.

A roar erupted from the dining creatures with more to follow. The grass crunched around her, but the creatures remained out of sight. She spun in a circle, trying to see which direction they were coming from as she went to grab her firearm, which was absent.

Dani groped her body for a weapon, anything she could use to defend herself, but came up empty-handed. The first creature leapt through the tall grass and landed on her, the two of them tumbling to the ground as another jumped on her, and another.

"Dani!"

Their teeth tore at her flesh on her side, causing it to burn and gush the violet-colored ooze.

"Dani!" Howard's voice pulled her out of the dream as he shook her. "Wake up!"

Dani clawed and thrashed, attempting to escape the perceived attack until Cruz pinned her to her bed. His strong grip held her down while Howard ran a cool cloth over her head and said something she couldn't quite understand to Cruz before the darkness came again.

Her mind continued to dance between consciousness and sleep as flashes of the planet, the creatures, her parents, and her crew came in random intervals. The intervals slowly grew longer and longer until she was able to wrap her mind around what was happening.

Various images started staying with her for longer periods of time. Howard and Jag arguing at the foot of her bed, Sylvine checking her wound and applying the concoction, Cruz with his arms around Cassia as she cried at Dani's bedside. Each vision was fleeting, and no matter how desperate Dani was to interact, she couldn't quite manage to do so.

The next time Dani woke up, she was nose-to-nose with a black, furry, vibrating weight on her chest. As her eyes fluttered open, Carl cocked his head and rubbed his face on hers. Dani sputtered and spit out the bits of cat fur that found their way into her mouth.

"Are you really awake?" Cassia sat up from her slouched position in the chair next to Dani's bed.

"Ugh, I think so. What happened?" She squinted in the dim lighting, her head pounding.

"You were injured. Best Cruz could figure was that it happened when Jag landed on you. We found some blood on his knife along with a little bit of that purple stuff."

Dani pushed herself up into a seated position, wincing and grabbing her side as Carl curled up on her lap. "Yeah, but that was nothing. How'd it turn into this?"

She lifted her shirt, her eyes widening at the vibrant purple markings that snaked like tendrils across her abdomen from beneath the fresh bandage.

"We think it was some kind of venom or virus from the creatures. It was pretty touch and go there for a while. Sylvine did something with some weird sap and flowers, and that's what finally helped pull you out of it."

"How long was I out?" Dani pushed herself up into a seated position. "Wait, how's Jag?"

Cassia smiled and nodded toward the door. "Ask him yourself."

Dani turned to see Jag leaning in the doorway. "You look like you're feeling better," he said as he approached her bed, limping, and sat on the foot of it.

"Yeah." Dani breathed a sigh of relief. "You too."

"Sylvine can work wonders with random plant bits and some spit." Jag chuckled. "As gross as that may be."

"So, wait, what's going on? Was I out long? Did we figure out where we are?" Dani raised a hand to where she'd hit her head. There was a tender bump, but no open wound.

"Slow down there." Jag got up and got Dani some water. "You've been in and out for the past three days."

"*Three days*? You're kidding me. Why so long?"

"Well, when you get poisoned and don't tell anyone about it, then it takes a bit to make you better." Jag glared as he spoke.

Dani cleared her throat. "Right, so update me on what's going on, please."

"Z's been keeping everyone in line. Cruz has spent all his time either looking after us or trying to figure out where we are. Sylvine is quite the medic, and Cassia's been taking care of everyone."

"So we're still lost." Dani sighed, sinking back against her headboard.

"For now, but we'll figure something out. We always do." Jag patted Dani's hand.

Cassia perked up. "I have made some progress logging Sylvine's language. I'm working on updating the translation programming so we can communicate more effectively."

"Okay, well, that's good ncws. Do we know anything about her yet?"

"She hates Carl," Jag said with a chuckle.

"She doesn't *hate* Carl." Cassia rolled her eyes with a huff. "She just doesn't *know* Carl."

Just then, Sylvine walked into Dani's room, looking down at a tray of medical supplies. The second she laid eyes on Carl, she gasped and turned around and left the room.

"What'd I tell ya?" Jag asked, folding his arms across his chest.

"That doesn't prove anything." Cassia dismissed his question with a wave of her hand.

A moment later Cruz returned with the tray and shooed Carl from the bed, handing the tray to Jag.

Carl hissed at Cruz before jumping down and winding his way around Cassia's legs.

"Oh, yeah, who couldn't love Carl?" Jag's voice dripped with sarcasm.

Cassia glared at him before scooping Carl up and leaving the room.

"You guys need to lighten up. Carl's not so bad," Dani interjected.

"*Time for your medicine,*" Cruz signed before preparing his supplies.

Uncharted Territory

Dani lay back and exposed the wound, allowing Cruz to clean it. At one point she winced, causing a look of concern to bloom on Jag's face. But before anyone could say anything, Zadria poked her head into the room.

"Cruz, I think we've got a hit on your location program!"

"That's great! Cruz, go. Jag can finish up here." Dani waved at Cruz to leave.

Cruz hurried out of the room after Zadria, and Jag placed the tray on Dani's legs, walking around the bed to take Cruz's place.

"You sure you want me to do this?" Jag asked as he examined the wound. "I don't want to hurt you."

"I'll be fine," Dani reassured him as their eyes met. "I'm tough."

Jag offered a crooked smile before picking up where Cruz left off. He carefully finished cleaning the wound before taking out some of the sap and flower mixture. He coated a section of gauze with the stuff and gently applied it to the wound.

Dani watched him closely, trying not to let the twinges of pain show in her expression. She didn't want him to feel bad when he was trying so hard to be tender with her. At one point, his hand brushed against her stomach and the smallest of gasps caught in her throat as his touch caused an electrified sensation to ripple through her body.

Jag quickly withdrew his hands. "Are you okay?" he asked, his eyes brimming with concern.

"Yeah." Dani blushed. "I'm fine. Go ahead."

She took a deep breath and lay back, focusing her attention on the ceiling. Her own reaction caught her off guard and she wasn't sure what to do about it, so instead she opted to pretend it didn't happen.

"Okay, you're all set." Jag sat back and smiled, admiring his handiwork.

"Great, thank you." Dani sat back up and took a deep breath, not sure what else to do in the uncomfortable growing silence. "I'd better go check in with Howard."

Jag nodded and helped Dani to her feet. "I'll check in with Z and Cruz to see where they are, or rather to see if they know where we are." He forced an awkward laugh as he left.

Uncharted Territory

Dani took careful steps out of her room. Her body was telling her she should stay in bed, but she knew she'd go crazy if she didn't get up and at least try to do something. Using the wall for support, Dani eventually made it to the engine room. Howard was inside, wearing a welder's helmet with the visor pushed up. He was bent over the jump drive with two pots from the kitchen next to him. "How's it going in here?"

"It's going," Howard answered with a sigh, keeping is head down. "I was wondering when you were going to wake up. How're you feeling?"

"I'll manage just fine," Dani assured him as she peeked inside one of the pots.

"I had to get the impurities out. Luckily for us, this element doesn't require an unimaginable level of heat. Though, we're not going to want to use these pots again."

"Z and Cruz think they may have figured out where we are. I'm checking in on them next."

Howard faced Dani and bit his lip. The confident mechanic didn't look so sure. "Finding out which direction we need to go is only part of the problem."

J. L. Stowers

Dani waited for Howard to finish his sentence and raised an eyebrow when he didn't. "So what's the other part?"

"Well, even with all the egniorium in the universe, I don't know that we'll make it."

Dani raised a hand to her throbbing head. She was starting to regret getting up. "Elaborate, please."

"I calculated the amount of egniorium our jump drive would be able to handle without blowing the entire ship to bits. But it's not enough to get us back to where we started."

"We don't need to get back to where we started," Dani interrupted. "We just need to get back to friendly territory."

Howard sighed audibly. "I'm not even sure that's possible. I mean, I'll do everything I can to get us as close as possible, but it may just not be something this ship can do with its current equipment."

"I see. Best case scenario?"

"Best case scenario, we go as far as the modified jump drive will take us. It doesn't explode. We end up in neutral territory and *Houston* picks us up."

"And I take it worst case scenario is the opposite of all of those things?"

150

Howard nodded as he carefully placed the cover back over the jump drive. "It's ready."

Dani took a deep breath and let it out slowly, her head still reeling. "I guess we better round up the crew."

Dani and Howard made their way to the bridge. Along the way, Howard shot Dani a few worried glances when she had to stop and lean against the wall for support.

"I'm fine, I promise," she tried to convince Howard and herself.

"Okay." Dani sighed as they finally entered the bridge. "Did we figure out where we are?"

Zadria was perky and excited. "We sure did! Cruz's program *finally* worked."

Cruz seemed mildly annoyed with the emphasis on 'finally,' but otherwise looked pleased with himself. "*We backtracked to our last known location and the program ran simulations for the shift in identifying stars and planetary systems at precise increments to account for our possible direction and distance. We're actually pretty lucky it hit so fast. With so many possibilities, it could have taken weeks, or even months.*"

"It's about time luck was on our side." Dani grinned and approached the holographic display. "Oh, maybe I spoke too soon."

"As you can see," Zadria started as Jag joined them, "the reason this area is uncharted is because we're beyond our borders. In fact, we're even beyond the Vaerian borders. It's probably a good thing we jumped out of that wormhole when we did because, otherwise, who knows how far out we would have ended up."

"So we have a heading?"

Zadria nodded. "Yes, and Cruz already plotted a path on the navigation system."

Cruz tapped some keys and brought up the plotted course.

"Great." Dani started to feel relief for the first time in a while. However, the feeling was fleeting as she saw the disappointment on Howard's face. "What are you thinking, Howard?"

Howard let out a deep sigh and scratched his chin. "It's going to be close. It might not be a bad idea to take our time and travel a ways before we try to jump in order to get as far as possible, because if we land short, we're going to stop right here, smack dab in Vaerian territory."

"We can do that." Dani nodded, leaning in to take a closer look at the Vaerian space Howard indicated.

"This... might be a bad time to mention this then," Cassia spoke out from the doorway with Sylvine at her side.

CHAPTER 9

"**W**hat is it?" Dani asked, dreading the answer.

"The medicine being used to treat both you and Jag is almost completely gone. From what I understand"—Cassia offered a reassuring smile to Sylvine—"she's been working on another type of medicine using the tongues of the beasts that she collected, but it might not work as well, if at all."

Dani took a deep breath. "Okay, so what's that mean for us?"

"Well, I'm not sure exactly. There's still a bit of a language barrier. But, it could mean that you both start to decline again. As long as this venom or poison is in your system, it will continue to cause problems. Sylvine mentioned you need the medicine until all the '*ninchak*' has been neutralized. She had enough of the ingredients to get Jag back to health, but..."

"Right." Dani trailed off, her heart sinking. Once again, her self-sacrificing efforts had caused more damage.

"Hey," Jag said quietly at her side. "Don't beat yourself up."

Her eyes met his, and instead of the anger she expected, there was a softness to them. He may not have been holding her latest mistake against her, but she was.

Dani cleared her throat. "Sylvine, do you need any help?"

"*Tærramol ćer anlĩng da?*" Cassia translated.

Sylvine hesitated, and Dani could see the gears turning in her head. "*Vot*," Sylvine replied, pointing at Cruz.

"Cruz and Cassia, go with Sylvine. The rest of you, stay here. We need to get going," Dani ordered before adding, "Howard, if you need to do anything else with the engines, then go ahead."

"They should be all set. We'll have to travel at sub-light speeds to preserve the modified jump drive until we're ready to use it. But don't push the engines too hard. We'll need them to be at least at fifty percent in order to perform a jump of this magnitude."

Dani nodded and took her seat as Jag, Howard, and Zadria did the same. "Got it."

Cruz and Cassia left the bridge to help Sylvine create the medicine, and Zadria began systems checks.

"Is there anything else we need before we leave this section of space?" Dani asked.

"I would have liked to collect some samples of the wildlife—"

"Are you kidding me?" Jag interrupted. "You have a death wish?"

"Uh... no. But it would be nice for the GC to log the creatures and prepare antidotes should anyone else encounter creatures like this. But there isn't time for that anyway."

"We can report the location and our findings to Patrick when we get back. I'm sure he'll use the information to determine what to do next, but in all honesty we may not be able to get back over here based on its location alone." Dani continued, "So if there's nothing else, I'm going to pull us out of orbit and start heading home."

Dani fired up the engines and turned *Osirion* away from the brightly colored planet, aligning with Cruz's plotted course. Once on track, she set the autopilot and sat back in her chair, watching as they flew past the other planets in the system. Many of them fell within the habitable zone and had great potential for colonization, provided they could get a handle on the wildlife. But Dani almost felt bad about reporting the system's location back to Patrick. If the GC did make a move on the territory, they'd likely colonize and mine it to the point of depletion as they had with many other systems.

It was such a quiet, peaceful system from this vantage point. War had not yet spread this far, though if any of the players knew what was out here then they'd inevitably make a play for it.

Their journey out of the planetary system was a quiet one. Dani glanced around at Jag and Zadria, wondering what thoughts danced through their minds as the last of the planets faded away behind them. Zadria's young eagerness kept her eyes locked on the screen while Jag dozed off in his seat.

"Z, I'm going to go check on the others. Please keep an eye on things."

"You got it, Ca—Dani."

Uncharted Territory

The doors to the bridge slid open, and a pungent odor hit Dani right in the face. "Ugh," she mumbled as she made her way to the kitchen, the source of the foul smell. Inside she found Sylvine, Cassia, and Cruz.

Cruz was loading lavender-colored liquid into a number of syringes while Sylvine stirred a large pot of the stuff. Cassia was putting together a tray of snacks for the crew and making fresh coffee.

"How's it coming in here? Aside from the smell." Dani wrinkled her nose.

"Good," Cassia chirped. "They're just getting everything set so we have the medicine ready if we get in a pinch."

Dani peered into the pot Sylvine was stirring. "How can the tongues of the creatures make an antidote when they're the ones that poisoned us in the first place?"

"It seems the creatures are susceptible to their own venom, so they possess a gland within the muscle of their tongue that secretes antibodies. I didn't understand it until Sylvine showed me the gland herself," Cruz signed and then pointed to a filleted tongue lying on the table. The tongue itself was the size of a dinner plate, with a bulbous sac inside.

"How'd she know all of this?" Dani questioned as she peered down at the tongue.

"My guess is that her kind has encountered these creatures before. But I'm still refining the linguistic program so I'm not completely certain. But, from watching her, I'd say she's done this before."

Sylvine turned and gestured for Dani to lift her shirt. Dani complied, and Sylvine bent down to examine the wound. The tendrils were smaller, but still present. She reached for a syringe and injected it near the wound.

Dani gritted her teeth at the pinch of the needle and the burning feeling that followed with the injection, but it passed quickly. "Well, hopefully she's not secretly trying to kill us off," Dani joked.

Cassia shook her head. "I don't know why she'd work so hard to bring you back to us if that was her plan."

"Guys." Zadria appeared in the doorway, panting. "Come quick. It's Jag."

Dani sprinted after Zadria back toward the bridge with Cassia, Cruz, and Sylvine close behind. Jag lay on the floor, with

Howard over him, performing CPR. Cruz quickly took over and continued compression and rescue breathing. Sylvine injected Jag with two syringes of the antidote while Dani watched on in horror, her hand placed over her mouth.

After several agonizing seconds, Jag coughed and began breathing on his own, Cruz checking his pulse.

Dani rushed to his side, kneeling beside him as his eyes fluttered open, then fell closed again. "What happened?"

"He had some kind of seizure and just was gone." Zadria stared at Jag in disbelief.

Dani stared at Jag's chest as it rose and fell with each breath.

"Let's get him to his room," Cruz signed.

The combined effort of the crew was enough to get Jag transported safely into his bed, Dani remaining at his side. "How bad is it?"

"It seems pretty bad," Cruz started. *"I checked the logs—he missed a dose of medication. There was only one dose left and he insisted we use it on you. I thought we'd have the new medicine done in plenty of time.*

I'm sorry, Dani. We'll keep a close eye on him."

Dani sighed and traced a finger over the back of Jag's hand while Zadria placed a cool, damp towel on his forehead and Sylvine examined the wound. The dark coloring on Dani's abdomen now encompassed Jag's entire leg. "We need to get him back to the *Houston.*"

She reluctantly dragged herself from Jag's room and returned to the bridge, where Howard was keeping an eye on the autopilot and other systems.

"Is the shithead going to be alright?"

Dani managed a slight smile; she knew Howard's comment was a term of endearment. Despite how much they bickered, Howard really did care about Jag, though Dani knew he'd never admit it. "I really hope so."

"I'm guessing you want to jump now?"

Dani nodded. "I think it'll be best for Jag."

"Howard stood and gave Dani's shoulder a squeeze. "I completely understand. I'd do the same. But what do we do about our guest?"

Dani pursed her lips. "I'll go find out."

After leaving the bridge, Dani found Cassia and Sylvine in the hall outside of Jag's room. Cassia was fitting a translation chip on Sylvine's shirt.

"Sylvine, we have to try to get home. You're more than welcome to stay with us."

As Dani spoke, the translation chip worked to translate her words for Sylvine. Unfortunately, Dani was unsure of how accurate the translation was, because Sylvine seemed to be slightly confused, and looked to Cassia.

"Oh, uh," Cassia mumbled as she poked at the tablet in her hand. "Try now."

"Sylvine, we are returning home. Would you like to travel with us?"

After the translation finished, Sylvine nodded. "*Pânulkûtna tha hîn azhken hi.*"

The chip answered, "Yes, I'd like to travel with you."

"Great." Dani was relieved they wouldn't have to stop or turn back to drop her off somewhere. "Cassia, can you and Sylvine stay back here and keep an eye on Jag? That will give you more time to work on the linguistic program as well. Learn what you can about her and her language."

"Yes, of course. I have my comm, if you need anything," Cassia replied.

Carl strolled down the hallway toward them, and Sylvine's eyes widened. He offered a passing glance to the three women as he continued on toward the bridge. Sylvine began rattling off too many words for the translation chip to handle and didn't calm down again until Carl was out of sight.

"It's okay," Cassia tried to reassure Sylvine, but her attempt failed as Sylvine retreated to Jag's room. Cruz and Zadria walked out past her, looking confused.

"I'm not sure why she doesn't like Carl, but we should probably try to keep him away from her. She really seems to get upset by him," Dani said.

Cassia sighed. "Alright. But if she'd just give him a chance—"

"We can revisit this later. For now, we need to get going."

Cassia nodded and returned to Jag's room as Dani made her way back to the bridge.

"Cruz, I'll need you to take Jag's seat for me while he's out of commission. You're the next in line and I know you've had experience with the weapons systems. Z and Howard, go ahead and take your normal stations. I'll let you know if I need your help with any other duties."

The group entered the bridge and took their respective seats, Dani grimacing as the harness of the captain's chair ran across her tender wound. She quickly accessed the ship's statistics to distract herself. "Looks like everything is fully charged and ready to go."

"*I've input the coordinates into the system,*" Cruz signed as he pulled the weapons relay down and adjusted it to his position.

"Ready to go, just give the word," Howard called out from his seat.

Dani took a deep breath and looked at the coordinates in the system. "How close are we going to get?"

"Couldn't tell you for sure, maybe half or two-thirds of the way."

Dani nodded. "Alright, Howard, let's see what she can do."

"Preparing to jump," Howard announced.

The normal hum of the jump drive was replaced by a wretched screeching noise that almost reminded Dani of the animals from the planet. She shot Howard a quick worried look, but he shrugged in return, then gave a thumbs-up.

Dani shook her head and turned to face the front again just as *Osirion* made the jump into hyperspace. The typically smooth transition was much rougher this time, the ship seeming to fight the jump drive. They lurched forward after a period of jerks, and the stars around them streaked into blurs.

"Is it supposed to be this rough?" Dani asked over the sound of the straining engines.

"It's not supposed to jump this far at all!" Howard shouted back.

Dani clutched the arms of her seat as *Osirion* began to shake violently. "She's going to come apart!"

Howard pursed his lips and pounded away on the keys, flipping through page after page of data and status updates. Cruz steadied the weapons relay as the shaking grew worse. Dani squeezed her eyes shut and focused all her attention on the ship as though her will alone would keep it held together.

Then, suddenly, the shaking stopped. Dani opened her eyes to a new scene. They were in a new system, gliding silently through the void between planetary giants with swirling cloud cover. "Well, we're not dead. That's a start."

Before she could finish her sigh of relief, alarms sounded throughout the bridge.

"Fire in the engine room!" Dani alerted Howard, who headed off to investigate.

"I'm picking up two ships ahead," Zadria announced. "One of which is Vaerian."

"Shit. Activating cloaking now." Dani switched on *Osirion*'s cloaking mechanism.

"You okay back there?" Dani asked through the comm.

"Yup, fire's out, just a little one. Jump drive might be shot though."

Dani sighed. "Of course."

She brought up the engine screen and was relieved to find that at least the sub-light engines and thrusters were fully operational. Dani quickly scanned the planetary system and decided to maneuver around to a moon orbiting a nearby planet. It was dangerous to fly out in the open when cloaked, as the risk for collision was much higher.

"Alright, Zadria, Cruz, let me know where we're at and what's nearby." Dani sank back in her chair, feeling faint.

Cruz made his way to his station and accessed the navigation systems while Zadria ran scans of the surrounding area.

"The planet and moon we're orbiting are barren; no lifeforms of any kind. The Vaerian ship is about to come into view."

Sure enough, as they made their way around the planet, a Vaerian ship became visible. It was still some distance away, but the massive ship still seemed threatening despite the distance.

"What's that?" Dani squinted at the bottom of the screen.

"Looks like someone's docked aboard the Vaerian ship, but it doesn't look like Vaerian technology at all. In fact, I've never seen a ship like that before." Zadria zoomed in on the craft.

The large industrial-looking Vaerian warship was dark, angular, and menacing, a stark contrast to the smooth, yellow, bubble-like ship docked in its lower bay. Dani searched for any identifying marks but found none. "Cassia, to the bridge please."

Dani knew that Cassia's extensive knowledge of other races might provide some clue as to who was consorting with their enemy.

Cassia entered the bridge, followed by Sylvine. "Jag's doing much better. I think the new medicine is working."

"Have you ever seen a ship like that before?" Dani nodded toward the screen.

Cassia stared at the screen momentarily before sitting at her station. "No, running some scans though. Do you know where we are?"

Dani didn't hear Cassia's question because she was too busy staring at Sylvine.

The redheaded warrior woman stood in the bridge, awash with confusion. She narrowed her eyes and peered at the smaller ship, a frown forming across her face.

"Do you know who that is?" Dani asked her.

Sylvine turned to face Dani. "*Donulkoshumnakirit thaji.*"

Dani frowned as the translation chip translated the phrase to 'We should go.'

Ding.

Cruz had projected the planetary system on the holographic display. Dani's eyes widened as she recognized it. "I'm with Sylvine. We need to get out of here. We're right smack dab in the middle of the Vaerian home system."

"That means that between us and GC territory lies the biggest Vaerian armada in existence." Zadria stumbled back into her chair.

"Yup, and we're on the *wrong side* of that blockade." Dani sighed. "Cruz, Sylvine, can you check on Jag?"

Cruz nodded and the pair left the bridge.

"Howard, I need you back here, now please."

"On my way, boss."

Dani fell back into the captain's chair. There were few places they could be that were worse than being deep in Vaerian territory, although flying face-first into a star was a close second.

"What's u—GAH!" Howard stumbled over Carl, who had made himself at home in the entrance of the bridge. He glared and muttered at the feline as it darted across the room and landed safely in Cassia's lap. "Damn cat."

"How's the engine room?"

"Actually, it wasn't bad at all. The fire was rather superficial. I even figure we have enough egniorium to try another jump if we need to, which might not be a bad idea considering..." Howard nodded to the screen, which now framed the Vaerian warship.

"Plus there's more where that came from." Dani gestured toward the holographic display.

"Oh my." Howard cringed as he turned back toward Dani. "You probably aren't going to like what I say next then."

"As long as it ends with us returning back to GC territory safely, I'm happy."

Howard shot a nervous glance around the bridge, then started picking at the grime on his hands.

"Okay, fine." Dani sighed. "Let's hear it."

"There is some leftover egniorium, thanks to Jag and his tendency to bite off more than he can chew. It's not a lot, but it'll get us closer to home."

Dani raised a brow. "That's good news. What's the catch?"

"Well, the jump drive is about fifty percent more likely to explode."

Dani rubbed her palm across her forehead. "Sounds like we can choose between trying to tiptoe our way through or jumping and hoping we don't blow ourselves to smithereens."

Her thoughts were interrupted as Cruz placed a road hand on Dani's shoulder, causing her to remove her hand from her face. "*He's awake.*"

"Z, watch the bridge. Make sure we don't break orbit or attract the attention of any Vaerian ships. I'll be right back."

Dani hurried down the hall into Jag's quarters with Cruz on her heels. Sylvine was at his bedside, checking his wound. "Do you two mind if we have a moment?" Dani asked, nodding toward the door.

Cruz nodded and beckoned Sylvine to follow him.

Dani exhaled loudly as she took the seat next to Jag's bed. "Hanging in there?"

"I think so," he mumbled through a weak smile and half-closed eyes. "What's going on out there?"

"Oh, you don't worry about that, Jag. I've got it all under control."

"Dani..." Jag warned with a glare.

Dani was surprised he had the strength to muster up such a stink eye in his current state. "We're in Vaerian territory, on the wrong side of the armada. We're cloaked, but we obviously can't stay here forever. Especially with us in this shape, I'm not sure how long the medicine will last."

"What are our options?"

"Well the first jump was pretty rough. We could do another, but it'd be risky. The other choice is to get as far as we can while we're cloaked. If we can't get past the armada, we can try a hop, but that won't get us out of their reach."

Jag winced as he shifted in his bed. The blanket fell away, and Dani could see that the purple was spreading further, the tendrils reaching up toward his abdomen.

"I'm going to tell Cruz to save the rest of the medicine for you. Your injury is much worse than mine."

Jag shook his head. "No, if anything, you should take the rest. The crew needs you. And I think you should go with the second option. Stay cloaked and get as far as you can. Then we'll figure it out when we get to the armada. It's safer than trying to jump from here. If we fail, then we're going to attract a whole lot of unwanted attention."

"Jag." Dani started and leaned in to take his hand. "If we do that, it's going to take much longer. Have you seen your leg?"

"Hey." He gave her hand a little squeeze. "It's okay, really. You know it's the best option for the crew. If I weren't sick, you wouldn't even be arguing with yourself right now. I'll be fine. Now get out there and get a move on."

Dani stared at Jag for a moment, not wanting to leave him in this condition. "I'll send Sylvine back to keep an eye on you."

He nodded and closed his eyes, his grip loosening on her hand.

Dani took his hand and placed it at his side, lingering to watch him breathe, terrified he would stop again at any moment. She eventually had to drag herself from the room and back to the bridge with a lump in her throat.

"Sylvine, please stay with Jag. Keep an eye on him," she said, gesturing back down the hall.

Sylvine nodded and left the bridge, looking relieved to get away from Carl, who was sitting on the floor a few feet away, staring at her and twitching his tail.

"We're going to stay cloaked and see if we can safely navigate back to GC territory," Dani said as she took her seat and ran through the system checks.

"But, Jag..." Cassia started.

"I know," Dani mumbled quietly. "Everything's in order. Let's get out of here."

Dani navigated *Osirion* away from the moon and along the course Cruz had plotted in the navigation system. She took a deep breath, relieved to be putting more distance between the Vaerian warship and themselves, but couldn't help but wonder what awaited them when they reached the armada.

"Dani!" Cassia's voice urgently called out. Even Carl retreated into the space near Cassia's feet at her station.

The sensors lit up red, indicating an incoming energy burst. "Hold on!" Dani hollered as she quickly strapped herself into her seat. *Osirion* shuddered, and the power flickered throughout the bridge. "What *was* that?"

"The Vaerian war ship... it's—" Cassia stammered.

"It's *gone!*" Dani finished her thought.

The space the Vaerian warship had occupied was now a mess of debris radiating outward at considerable speed. The crew stared in awe of the utter annihilation of the massive, armored vessel. Even under heavy fire, they didn't just burst apart like that.

"It must have blown up from the inside," Dani muttered as she stared at the screen.

Sylvine ran back into the bridge and gasped, clamping her hand over her mouth.

Ding, ding, ding.

The incessant ringing and clanging coming from Cruz's station finally pulled her attention as he frantically signed, "*Cloaking is down!*"

"What?" Dani dove into her console and brought up the cloaking mechanism, desperately trying to activate it again. "Shit, the explosion must have damaged it. Howard, can we jump?"

"We can in a minute!" Howard sprinted out of the room, making good time for his size and age.

"Incoming Vaerian battleship. They're charging weapons," Cassia announced.

"Evasive maneuvers! Cruz, I need you on weapons!"

"Incoming transmission."

"Half-screen, please, Cassia."

The face of a high-ranking Vaerian appeared on the screen—and he didn't look happy. Every breath he took echoed throughout the bridge as he stared down Dani and her crew. The slits on his neck were done in a way Dani had never seen. Commanders typically had three slits on either side of their neck. This Vaerian had eight, six horizontal and two vertical. His horns were also much more prominent than Dani had ever seen. The translation of their alien language rolled across the bottom of the screen.

Your presence is a direct violation of the current cease-fire between the Vaerian Nation and the Galactic Conglomerate.

J. L. Stowers

Furthermore, your attack on our craft where peaceful negotiations were being conducted shows a total disregard for the diplomatic process. As a result, your ship shall now be destroyed.

"Whoa, hang on, we didn't attack anyone! We are actually here by mistake and trying to get home," Dani tried to explain.

The Vaerian snorted before continuing on.

Your trespass alone is an act of war.

Then he blipped off the screen while Dani sat and quickly diverted full power to their shields. "Cruz, don't fire, there's no way we can take that ship out. We're outgunned."

Howard huffed and puffed back into the bridge. "It's... ready... to go."

Osirion shook as a blast from the battleship struck their shields, the energy spidering out from the initial point of contact as it dispersed across the shields. Howard stumbled in front of his station, but managed to crawl up and clip into his harness.

"Powering jump drive!" Dani shouted as another burst from the Vaerian weapons shook *Osirion*. "Sylvine, Cruz's station, now!"

Uncharted Territory

Dani wasn't sure if Sylvine understood her command, so she frantically pointed at Cruz's unoccupied seat, and that seemed to get her point across, because Sylvine scrambled over to the seat.

Osirion jerked and tossed, the power flickering once more and alarms sounding. Dani and her crew were thrown back in their seats, then forward again in what felt like the absolute worst carnival ride of all time. Dani was actually thankful that she hadn't eaten anything in quite some time; otherwise she was sure she'd be wearing it.

She clung to the arms of her chair like Carl clung to Cassia's lap, judging by Carl's hissing and Cassia's cries of pain. Dani could only hope that Jag was holding up in the back. The shaking intensified, and the lights and consoles in the bridge went out as the inertia threw them forward abruptly against the harnesses in their seats.

"Is it over?" Zadria's shaky voice sounded from across the bridge as the lights began to flicker on. The poor girl gripped her tablet to her chest, looking quite frazzled.

"I'm not sure. Cruz, as soon as systems are up, can you please figure out where we are?"

The absence of the bell's ding drew Dani's gaze toward Cruz. The somber expression on his face as he stared at the screen said it all.

"You already know, don't you?"

Cruz nodded slowly before turning to face Dani. *"We're in the Dead Zone."*

THANK YOU!

Thank you for taking the time to read the third installment of the Ardent Redux Saga.

I've had a lot of fun with this series and I'm hoping you'll love it as much as I do.

If you enjoyed Uncharted Territory, please consider leaving a review. Reviews tell me which books my readers enjoy most so I can continue to make them a priority.

Please follow me on Facebook at:
www.facebook.com/jlstowersofficial

Or visit my website at www.jlstowers.com for the latest updates, promotions, and giveaways.

OTHER BOOKS BY J. L. STOWERS

Made in the USA
Middletown, DE
04 March 2023